Broken Women

A Lesbian Love Story

Anne Hagan

To all the Women of the Lesbian Book Writers, Readers Group, the Lesbian Book Readers Club and the Lesbian Book Nook; thank you for your friendship, support and encouragement over the past 18 months.

Broken Women

PUBLISHED BY:
Jug Run Press, USA
Copyright © 2016

https://annehaganauthor.com/

This is a work of fiction. Names, characters, places and incidents are products of the author's imagination or are actual places used in an entirely fictitious manner and are not to be construed as real. Any resemblance to actual events, organizations, or persons, living or deceased, is entirely coincidental.

Broken Women

Table of Contents

Part One
Barb and Lisa

Chapter 1

Barb and Lisa
Steamboat Springs, Colorado
Thursday Night, March 28th, 2013

"The Blue Moon is out Kane. Can you go back and change it please?"

"Sure thing boss lady." He sauntered down the length of the back bar and disappeared behind the swinging door to the kitchen.

I scanned the half square of the bar top just in time to catch two more men coming in. They came to a stop at a small gap between customers on the far end, the taller of the two waving a twenty in the air. I moved toward them.

"Welcome to Steamboat Willie's, gentlemen." I greeted them with a smile I was starting to feel less and less as the night drug on. "What can I get you?"

"Two Blue Moon draughts, please," the taller one requested.

"Oh, sorry. It will be a few minutes. I'm having it changed out right now. Do you want to wait or is there something else I can get you instead?"

He looked at his friend who was so busy bopping his head around to the mix the DJ was spinning and eying the guys around him, he was oblivious to our little exchange. He nudged the shorter man but, when he didn't get an immediate response from him, he told me,

"We'll wait," and handed me the twenty. After making him change, I readied two talls with orange slices and left them by the tap.

Lisa came out of the kitchen and, spying me, headed right for me. Touching my shoulder, she leaned in and spoke directly into my ear, "If you'd have called back, I could have changed that keg out."

"You don't need to be doing that stuff," I told her. "Besides, that hookup's a little tight. If we want to offer Kane the opportunity to manage this place, we need him to see every little nuance he's in for."

My wife nodded. "You're right, I suppose." She looked around. "Nice to see the place so packed on a Thursday."

"I'll tell you what, I'm already whipped. If the weekend is going to be like this, we're going to have to call in reinforcements."

"What's that you say?" Kane asked, returning.

"It's so busy," Lisa repeated for his benefit. "We're probably going to need more help for the weekend."

He nodded. "The only gay bar in town for Outboard Week...bound to happen, but we got this."

Marveling at his enthusiasm, I responded as I pulled the two beers, "Well still, if you have any buddies that want to earn a little extra cash this weekend schlepping drinks, you're welcome to give them a call."

He waved me off. "They'll drink more than they bring in. My uncle Roger might be willing to help out though, if he can stay behind the bar and mix drinks, that is. I'll work the floor more, if he'll do it."

Relief flooded my own features and Lisa nodded her approval too. "It's a deal," I told him. "Whatever hours he's willing to spare."

"You just need to get over your damn self, sweetie! You aren't all that, you know." The thin, bespectacled man stood and jabbed a finger at his table mate.

"Says you!" the other man said as he half rose too. "I could have any guy in this place and you know it!" He gripped the table edge to steady himself in place.

"Is that right, girl? I hardly think so."

"Just watch and learn then."

"What, are you going to do; go around offering blow jobs to every fella in the place? Huh?"

"So what if I do?"

"Gentlemen, how are we this fine evening?" Kane asked the two men as he stepped up to the little table and effectively got between them.

The guy wearing glasses looked the bartender up and down. "Well aren't you a cutie," he said, turning on the charm. "What's your name?"

Kane gave him a lopsided grin. "Thanks; and I'm Kane. So, is this your first trip to Steamboat?" He glanced back and forth between the two of them.

The second man released his grip from the table edge and eased back down in his chair as he answered, "Yes, actually. We were in Aspen for ski week last year but it seems a little friendlier and less...pretentious here."

"We pride ourselves here on hospitality and good powder. Actually, it's called the champagne of powders."

"The skiing was *amazing*," the first man replied as he resumed his own chair.

"Besides that, just wait till tomorrow. There's a virtual who's who coming into town. And, if all the celeb spotting on the slopes isn't enough, we're going to have live music here on Saturday night." He raised his hands to cup his mouth and he lowered his voice as he whispered conspiratorially, "Rumor has it that 'Adele' may take the mike for a song or two. That's just between us though, okay?" He raised an index finger to his lips in the universal sign of a secret just passed on.

"Adele!" the glasses wearing man practically screeched causing Kane to tap his finger against his lip several more times. In a lower tone, the other man continued, "I love me some Adele!"

"You'll have to join us Saturday then." He smiled again at them both.

"Oh honey, we'll be here with bells on!"

5

"We're damn lucky to have Kane on our team, Barb. He's sharp, friendly and the customers seem to love him," Lisa intoned from across the desk where I was sitting creating a purchase order for booze we were sure to be out of by Monday. "He defused a little spat out there without flexing a muscle and without having to give away any free drinks."

"What I like," I said, "is that he doesn't mix business with pleasure. He keeps his head about him when he's on the job...both of them."

Lisa grinned at that. "That has been a problem for us, hasn't it?"

"In a few of the bars we've rehabbed," I reminded her, "gay and straight. Remember that mixed dance club we had in Indy? That guy we had to let go there was a rapist in waiting."

"Don't remind me!"

I sat back in my chair and slumped down a little. "What's up out front now?"

"It's winding down. Skiing all day and dancing all night must not be in the cards for tonight."

I looked at the wall clock; 1:17 AM. "We'll have Hexx announce last call at 1:30 and then spin one more long mix."

"I'll tell him." She got up to go.

Something popped into my head. "Hey babe, in all the commotion tonight, I forgot to ask; any word from that guy in Portland?"

6

"Nadda." She sucked in her bottom lip for a second in the face she always made when she was concentrating. "I'll give him a call Monday. Our work here is about done. We need a new project."

Chapter 2

2:30 AM, Friday Morning, March 29ᵗʰ, 2013

"What a night!" Lisa groaned as she dropped her car keys on the stand beside the front door.

"Yeah; I really hate to say it, but I'll be glad when this week is over. I think every prima-donna skier in the country is already in town this week."

Lisa smiled back at me ruefully. "Hungry?" she asked.

I shook my head. "Just a glass of wine for me. I snuck a bite in between waves tonight but I really need to unwind."

"Is that right?" She touched my shoulder out of habit and this time gave it a squeeze as she passed me and headed toward the kitchen.

"Mmm, a backrub would be nice too."

"Oh really," Lisa tossed over her shoulder. "What's in it for me?"

I attempted to waggle my eyebrows at her suggestively but, when I got a laugh in response, I assumed the gambit failed.

Turning away, I moved into the living room and popped the television on for a little background noise. Pressing down on the volume key first I stopped, finger hovering over the button, as the channel the TV had been on went from commercial back to the movie that had been playing, 'Dirty Dancing', one of my

8

favorites. Moving to the sofa, I plunked down mindlessly, already caught up in the familiar story.

My Lisa and I sipped our wine as we watched Baby's older sister Lisa on the screen make a fool of herself at the talent show rehearsal and we both cringed during the scene where the little weasel wannabe manager, Neil, fingered Johnny for stealing Mo Pressman's wallet.

At the commercial break, I turned and said to my wife, "We should really get to bed. Tomorrow is going to be another long day. The whole weekend will be long..."

"It's almost over," she replied as she flipped a hand toward the flat screen.

I smiled to myself, happy that she loved the movie as much as I did. "True; and the end is the best part."

Lisa simply nodded.

Several minutes later, we both called out, "Nobody puts Baby in a corner!" and then laughed at each other.

As Swayze and Grey took the stage for their last dance as Baby and Johnny, Lisa set her wine glass down, stood and offered me her hand. "Dance with me?"

She pulled me to my feet and moved us out into the center of the room. Dancing with her was a favorite pleasure of mine.

Lisa took up a position behind me and, holding one of my hands, much as Patrick held

Jennifer's, she ran her other hand down the side of my breast as he did the same to Grey on screen. A delicious shiver ran up my spine and I started to shudder but then I was spinning away, caught in the dance.

Now I've had the time of my life
No, I never felt like this before
Yes, I swear it's the truth
And I owe it all to you

'Cause I've had the time of my life
And I owe it all to you

I've been waiting for so long
Now I've finally found someone to stand by
me
We saw the writing on the wall
As we felt this magical fantasy

So True, I thought. So true.

Now with passion in our eyes
There's no way we could disguise it secretly
So we take each other's hand
'Cause we seem to understand the urgency

Just remember
You're the one thing
I can't get enough of
So I'll tell you something
This could be love because

Broken Women

This is love...no doubt in my mind.

I've had the time of my life
No, I never felt like this before
Yes, I swear it's the truth
And I owe it all to you

Hey, baby!

With my body and soul
I want you more than you'll ever know
So we'll just let it go
Don't be afraid to lose control, no

Yes, I know what's on your mind
When you say, "Stay with me tonight" Lisa
bent in and stole a kiss.
Stay with me
And remember

You're the one thing
I can't get enough of
So I'll tell you something
This could be love because

I've had the time of my life
No, I never felt like this before
Yes, I swear it's the truth
And I owe it all to you

'Cause I had the time of my life

And I've searched through every open door
Till I found the truth
And I owe it all to you

Our own dance was a bit simpler than the one we were now only half watching but we only had eyes for each other. Lisa dipped me as Johnny lifted Baby. Then, finally, as the kids on screen moved into the crowd to take up dance partners, she stopped our own little mambo and moved in for another kiss, this time more than the quick buss that had caught me by surprise mid-way through the song.

She started slow, gently brushing my lips with hers and nipping a bit at my bottom lip but moving with her to the music had heightened all of my senses. I was on fire and I took control.

I could smell the faint remnants of the perfume she applied hours before. It fueled my arousal.

As we continued to kiss, I moved one hand to the clingy top covering her breasts. Finding a nipple already peaked and pushing out, I kneaded it with my fingers until Lisa moaned with the ache of her need.

I pulled her into me tighter with one hand while I raised the other away from her breast to stroke through her long, raven hair. She broke our kiss and buried her head in my shoulder as I combed through the strands like I'd done so many times before.

Naked now, in our bed, I brought Lisa's nipples back to stiff erectness, my tongue moving around and around her swollen aureoles. I caught her nipples with my teeth and pulled gently on them, nipping them slightly. Lisa groaned.

I moved down her body slowly, licking her skin and then kissing her belly. I stroked her stomach gently with my tongue and then I moved further to her thighs. She mewed and writhed on the sheets as I moved my head upward after only a few moments to run my tongue up and down her slit. She let her thighs spread for me and she tangled her fingers in my hair to guide me.

From between her thighs, I looked up at her in the dim light. Her beautiful face was aglow with the light of our lovemaking. I held the eye contact with her as my fingers delicately spread her lips further and caressed her.

"Please baby, please..."

Dipping my head low again, I leaned in and sucked her clit and laved it with my tongue. Lisa screamed out in her pleasure.

I stroked at her clit for a long time and then I slid my tongue into her center and sucked in her sweet juices. She tasted divine.

Her hips bucked and thrust upward. Moving a hand from its grip on her thigh, I ran my fingers over her wet center, then slowly inserted two inside her and rotated them in and out.

Licking and sucking her clit while I finger fucked her slowly, sent her into a frenzy.

"Faster baby, faster!" she begged.

She cried out as she came. I didn't stop. Picking up the pace even more, my hand was a blur as I slid my fingers in and out of her. She climaxed again, quickly, and then again. Then I slipped my fingers from her center and slowly licked her again. She gave a shudder as the tip of my tongue barely grazed her clit and she came again quickly. I moved up her body kissing it softly as I went. Pulling her into my arms, I held her and kissed her neck and the curve of her shoulder while she regained her breath.

"I love you Barb," she told me then.

"Not as much as I love you."

Chapter 3

10:00 AM, Friday, March 29th, 2013

Lisa tried to creep out of bed. I'd been curled into her so the withdrawal of her warmth roused me from slumber.

"Where are you going?"

"Bathroom."

"Are you coming back?"

"Mm, I'm kind of hungry."

While she went on about her business, I sat up and ran a hand through my hair. *After the night we had,* I thought, *I probably look a fright.*

Since Lisa was using our on-suite, I got up, grabbed sweats and headed for the guest bathroom where I took care of my own needs and tried to arrange my hair into some semblance of order.

When I emerged, she hadn't come out of our bedroom yet so I decided I'd start the foraging in the kitchen.

As I rounded the breakfast island, the blinking message light on the phone caught my eye. I punched the play button and then opened the fridge to peer inside while the mechanical lady voice began reeling off her usual spiel.

A more melodious woman's voice was up on the first message, "This message is for Lisa

Falk. This is Chastity with Dr. Welle's office. Please give us a call to make an appointment at your earliest convenience." Lisa walked into the room as the voice on the machine was leaving the number.

"Hey babe, that's the doctor's office. Your test results must be back. They want you to call them."

"Oh?" She raised an eyebrow. "What did they say?"

"Well nothing much on the machine; just a tech making the calls."

Lisa played the message back, wrote down the number and then dialed. After a brief, terse, conversation with whoever answered, she dropped her miffed tone and said into the receiver, "That'll be fine," then she hung up.

"What's going on?" I asked her.

"They want to see me A.S.A.P.," she spelled it out, "and they had an opening for 2:30 today so I guess I'm going in then."

"*We're* going in then."

"Babe, you don't need to go with me. It's probably nothing. Just stress. We've been going a hundred miles an hour lately getting this bar going and continuing to manage the others long distance. There's no need for you to go to hear how I need to rest more, yada, yada, yada. Besides, this is the biggest ski weekend of the year, as far as the bar is concerned. I'll be there as soon as they finish

16

telling me I need to start taking better care of me."

"There's a small mass in your cervix."

"Mass?"

Dr. Welle nodded. "Possibly a tumor. That could explain your tiredness and your general malaise."

"A tumor?" Lisa gulped, her fear evident on her face.

"It's not time to be alarmed just yet," Welle held a cautioning hand up. "We'll want to do a biopsy just as soon as we can and have the tissue tested. If it's benign, we have no real problem."

"And if it's...it's..."

"Malignant?" At Lisa's slight nod, the doctor continued, "then you'll need surgery to have it removed before it metastasizes elsewhere."

"Would you be doing the surgery?"

"First things first, Lisa. I'll perform the biopsy here at Yampa and then send the tissue I take out for testing. If you need surgery, I'll refer you to a specialist in Denver. We're not equipped to perform anything but routine procedures here."

"How soon for the biopsy?"

"The sooner the better."

###

"Cancer? I knew I should have gone with you!"

Lisa blew out a breath. "She kept cautioning me not to jump to conclusions yet. We won't really know anything for sure until after the biopsy, Monday."

"How quick do you get results back from something like that?"

"She said a couple or three days."

I got up and moved around my desk to my wife. "I love you Lisa Louise," I told her as I pulled her up out of her chair and into my arms. Whatever it is, we'll get through it together."

Chapter 4

I couldn't sit. I was up, pacing the floor in the surgical waiting room. Hours had passed since they'd taken her back but I didn't even know if she was in the OR yet. The electronic billboard that was there to keep families informed of their patient's status hadn't changed in Lisa's case in nearly three hours.

A volunteer came into the room pushing a cart. People jumped from their seats and lined up for coffee, fruit and cookies. Mindlessly, I fell into line too. When it was my turn, the cheerful young woman waited patiently while I decided that I only wanted water.

"How about an apple, Miss? That'll perk you up some," she coaxed me.

"I'm way past the age where people can legitimately call me 'Miss'," I said to her. Noting her puzzled look, I decided it wasn't worth pursuing and that I would just be holding up the line. "I'll take an apple, then."

Moving off to a seat in a corner near the conference room doors, where I could still see the billboard but where no one else seemed to want to sit, I flopped into a chair and started to work on the fruit.

I was nearly finished when the woman from the information desk in the hallway walked in

20

through an entry near me and called out, "Hawley family?" She waited while three people stood and gathered themselves and then moved over to her.

"Conference room one," she told them, pointing at a door just steps from my seat. "The surgeon will be there in just a couple of minutes. He's scrubbing out now." The little group moved toward the room, their relief at their wait being over, evident.

"Excuse me ma'am," I stood and asked the staffer as she turned to leave again, "Any word on Lisa Falk? I mean, there've been no updates." I swung an arm toward the billboard.

"I'm sorry, no. There are no updates at this time." And then, she was gone.

I sank back down. Five minutes passed that seemed like an eternity.

I've got to stop watching the clock...

Another ten minutes went by and then the door to room one opened. Expecting to see the Hawley crew coming back out, I was instead surprised to see a surgeon and an RN in clean scrubs standing there. "Falk family; anyone here for Falk?" the surgeon called out.

"I am," I said, rising. Relief washed through me that the wait was finally over and I'd get to see my wife soon.

Wordlessly both turned back into the small room. I followed. The female RN indicated I should take a seat.

I was anxious and didn't want to sit anymore. "How is she? How did it go?" I questioned the man I assumed performed Lisa's surgery.

"Ms.?" he peered at me as he questioned my identity.

"Falk-Wysocki – Barbara Wysocki. I'm Lisa's legal wife but I uh...never actually legally changed my name." I held up my left hand to display my wedding band. He didn't bat an eyelash.

"Please have a seat Ms. Wysocki." His tone was muted and that concerned me. I looked between the two of them but their features gave nothing away. Quietly I sat, dread starting to fill me. The RN took a seat right next to me as he leaned back against the door from the back hallway and started to speak again.

"I'm Philip Knox, the Chief of Surgery here at the hospital. One of our best surgeons was operating on Lisa today, Dr. Simmons. I regret to inform you that we lost her. Lisa passed during the procedure."

"What? What are you saying?"

The RN reached over and took my hand. "She's gone," she told me. "Lisa died during the surgery."

"What?" I was screaming now. "How? How is that possible?" I was shaking with fear and rage. *This can't be happening!*

"I assure you, we did everything we could," he tried to tell me. "When it became apparent that Lisa was in distress, I was called in. I stepped in to assist myself. I'm so sorry. We couldn't save her."

"What happened in there? You have to tell me what happened!" I looked at him and watched as he dropped his head, his chin almost touching his chest. Turning then, I looked at the nurse who was still holding my hand. "One of you better start talking!"

Knox picked up a chair near the back hallway door and, after covering the six or seven feet between us, placed it down right in front of me and sat. He leaned forward and looked directly at me. "I'll be reviewing all of the case notes, charts, and the video log but here's what I think happened. Please mind you, at this point it's just an educated guess."

I nodded, "Go on." My eyes welled up then as reality started to sink in. Tears began to roll. The nurse reached for a tissue box and held it out to me. I took one but I left the tears to fall and waited for him to speak again.

"We had an emergency procedure come in that bumped Lisa's removal procedure back a little bit. She waited in surgery prep for a couple of hours longer than she otherwise would have. During the procedure, I believe – this is just my thoughts without a full review – Lisa suffered a spell of deep vein thrombosis which caused a blood clot. The clot moved quickly to her lung and caused a pulmonary embolism."

"What does that mean in English?"

"The clot...or clots, blocked the flow of blood to her lungs and possibly even to her heart and brain. We couldn't break them up."

"This deep vein thing; that has something to do with her having to wait?"

"It's possible but not very likely. We administer Heparin before surgery to counteract clotting and we normally continue it even after surgery for patients at risk for clotting from being held motionless for long periods of time. I mention the wait because it did happen but Heparin is fail proof."

Our house already felt empty. At first, I moved about it with unseeing eyes. At some point in the early evening, I noticed it was snowing hard outside. I was drawn to the long windows to peer at the strange April storm blowing beyond.

I don't know how long I stood there, but finally, growing cold with the draft, I turned away. Before me spread the rustic beauty of the log home we'd traded for when we'd sold our last bar in Chicago and taken on the Willie's project.

Most of the black and glass furniture Lisa had loved so much for the townhouse we'd had in Chi Town was in a storage unit back there now. It just wasn't a fit for this place and we hadn't wanted to transport it all the out here anyway. Still, as I looked about, I saw so many books and photos and objects we'd bought together as we crisscrossed the country buying and rehabbing failing bars with promise and then reselling them and moving on.

I moved about now, touching this and that and remembering...just remembering. There was the brick we'd gotten when we went to our first ever – and only – NASCAR race when we were in Indy. It lay on a side table now like a paperweight for the mail.

There was the photograph taken from the camera attached to the Ferris wheel on the boardwalk in Myrtle Beach not long after it officially opened. I smiled at the memory as I looked at Lisa's laughing face.

In the kitchen, hanging from a rack over the center island, were the copper bottomed pots and pans that cost the moon but that she insisted I have just because I said I liked them. Tears started to well up again as I thought of the meals we'd both made and shared the last few years using them.

Our house phone rang. Lisa had always insisted on having a landline wherever we'd lived as a default business line. As I moved toward it, my eyes landed on a cut crystal vase resting on a sideboard by our little breakfast table. Ignoring the phone, I went to it instead, feeling compelled to touch it. I bought Lisa flowers for our first Valentine's Day together. As I ran my fingers over the bumpy texture, I remembered that she'd had nothing to put them in. Our dinner date had turned into a shopping trip to Macy's instead for the piece. We celebrated Valentine's Day at the mall food court over quick serve Chinese food.

The phone stopped ringing and voicemail picked up. My mother's voice came on the line.

"Barb, baby, I'm so sorry. We were at appointments all day for dad. We just got your message. Sweetie? Are you there? Sweetie, pick up please if you're there."

Letting out a breath as I reached for the phone I'd headed toward when the voicemail came on, I spoke into the receiver, "Hi mom; how's Dad?"

"Struggling, as always but that's not why we're calling...I'm calling. He's asleep. It's been a long day for him. What on earth happened out there? Tell me it isn't true!"

"It's true...I wish it wasn't." I relayed the little bit of information I had.

"Oh Barb, honey, how very awful. I...I...I don't know what to say."

"They'll be doing a full autopsy to get at the actual cause of death. I've been told her...her body will probably be released Thursday. The funeral will probably be Friday or Saturday."

It was quiet on the other end of the line. After a prolonged silence, I asked, "Mom, are you still there?"

"Yes, yes. I'm sorry. I'm just contemplating who I can get to come and stay with your father so I can come out for the funeral."

"You don't have to come out here. Stay there with dad."

"I should be there with you; I really should."

"How is he? You never told me."

"He isn't doing so well. They keep adjusting his heart medication but, so far, they haven't seemed to hit on the right combination. He's tired all the time and he complains constantly that he can't seem to catch his breath."

"Mom, just stay there with him. I'll manage just fine here. It will be a very small service here with just some local friends we've made in the six months or so we've been out here."

"What about her family?"

"There's none to speak of that would come here. She only had a few scattered cousins left, to speak of. Her parents are both long gone, remember?" I continued, "She didn't have any siblings. The aunt who raised her is gone now too. We buried her a couple of years ago."

"I remember that, now. Such a shame that she had no one else."

"She had me mom...she had us. Lisa always said we were all the family she ever needed anyway."

My mother sniffled at the other end of the line.

"Mom?" I prodded her gently.

"Yes?"

"Thank you."

"For what dear?"

"For loving and accepting me and Lisa too."

Broken Women

Chapter 5

Saturday afternoon, April 13th
Steamboat Willie's

"It was a nice service," Kane's Uncle Roger said from his perch on the bar stool next to mine.

"Thank you for coming. I appreciate you being there." I meant the words but I felt like I was speaking from outside my own body. It had been a rough week all around and a very emotional morning.

Kane himself moved toward us. "And you as well, thank you too," I told him.

He gave me a tight lipped grin and a nod in response. He pointed to my coffee cup and I nodded back at him to go ahead and refill it. The bar was closed for the day but several of us had naturally seemed to drift that way after the funeral.

"If you don't mind me asking," Roger began hesitatingly, "what will you do now? Will you stay on here or will you keep on moving about and doing rehabs?"

"That, I can't answer for sure. The rehabs are in my blood but it's all up to the courts and how big of a cut out of Lisa's estate they take."

He quirked an eyebrow in my direction, his question obvious on his face.

"Lisa and I were legally married in the eyes of the federal government but we weren't in the eyes of the State of Colorado. We have a registered Civil Union here which doesn't seem to mean much when it comes to probate. There are three bars that we kept in her name for tax purposes that are now going to be all caught up. We would use the income from those and the sale of more recent properties to buy the next place."

"Such a shame, that. So, no will leaving those to you?"

"There's a will."

"I don't understand then," he said, shaking his head. "Probate isn't required for wills, only for the lack of one. You can leave your assets to anyone you want if you have a will. Do you have a lawyer?"

"Yes." It was my turn to appear puzzled. "We actually use a firm that's got offices around the country since we move around so much."

"I'd be talking to them soon, if I was you. Get that will looked at and those assets transferred to you."

Wednesday, April 17th
Meecham and Seer Law offices
Denver, Colorado

"It's not quite so simple Ms. Wysocki," the junior lawyer was telling me, his tone borderline exasperated.

"What's so hard about it? I guess I'm just not understanding. It's a valid will. Lisa's estate shouldn't even be in probate."

"It may very well be but it's being contested as invalid."

"By whom? The state?"

He shook his head. "By a group claiming to be Lisa's rightful heirs; a Hake Swogger, a Heath Swogger and a Heidi Lykins. Are you familiar with them?"

"Well isn't that fast?" I was livid.

"How so?"

"I'm vaguely familiar with them. They're Lisa's cousins by marriage and her only living relatives. I took the time to bother to notify the two I could track down, Hake and Heidi who still live in Iowa where Lisa was from, about her death and the funeral but they couldn't even be bothered to send so much as a card let alone show up."

"So they're first cousins, then?"

I nodded. "Is that important?"

"You said they were her only living relatives so, in the event there was no will, they would be her legal heirs in the eyes of the state."

"And again, there is a will. How can they contest it?"

"They can contest anything they want to. It will be up to the court to determine if their claim is valid."

"Even if they don't live in Colorado?"

"Their relative location has no bearing on their claim."

"What are my chances here?"

"We're not in the business of laying odds Ms. Wysocki. If you wish to retain us to represent you in this matter, we'll work to serve your best interests."

May 2ⁿᵈ, 2013

"I don't know what to do mom; I feel like I'm drowning."

"Is there anything we can do to help?" her voice came back across the line.

"I appreciate that, but no. Just listening is enough."

"Fill me in, baby. What's going on?"

"The probate court out here froze all of the assets of Lisa's estate pending their final decision. That could take months. Meanwhile, her medical bills are still piling up."

"But, she had health insurance..."

I cleared my throat to keep from swearing into the phone with my disgust over our insurers. Instead I told her, "She did, yes, but she had a high deductible and it was a cost shared plan too; in other words, worthless. Since the funeral, I've run though what was left of the life insurance proceeds trying to pay off the medical bills but there's just no end."

"You would think when someone passes during a procedure that they would just...I don't know...but not bill you, that's for sure!"

There really wasn't a response for that and mom was on a roll anyway.

"You could just do what I do with your father's stuff; send them twenty dollars every time they send you a bill. They'll see you're making an attempt to pay and..."

"That isn't going to work. Some of these bills are for thousands of dollars."

"Oh."

"Once this case is decided, hopefully, I'll be able to tap the cash flow that's in holding right now, pay off the bills, pay off my lawyers and try to put my life back together...somehow, maybe...I don't know. Right now, I feel like I'm circling the drain."

Chapter 6

"They're offering to settle."

"They can take their offer and shove it. I don't owe them a thing and Lisa sure didn't either; bunch of blood suckers..."

"Now just wait, hear me out." Frazier Cross, the young lawyer who'd been dogging the case for the past couple of months, held up a hand to me. "This very well may not go our way. We may want to give serious consideration to a settlement offer."

"You've heard something you're not telling me, haven't you?"

"No, no. Nothing like that."

I caught the nervous shake of his hand as he pushed his glasses up a little on the bridge of his nose. "Why do I feel like I'm about to get royally screwed then?"

Cross cleared his throat but his voice still cracked a little when he spoke. "Ms. Wysocki, when Ms. Falk made out her last will and testament, it was just after the two of you married, correct?"

"Yes. We both did wills at the same time. You have to be careful when your marriage isn't universally recognized...fat lot of good that it did us." I couldn't see where this was going but he was quick to fill me in.

"At the time, there was one bar owned in her name. It was not specifically named to you in her will. It simply refers to 'business assets'; nothing more detailed."

"That's because we had no way of knowing at that time what business assets we would have control of at a given point in time, should either one of us pass on."

He was quiet.

"Are you saying we should have named everything and updated our wills every time something changed? Because we didn't, its coming back to bite me?"

"In an ideal world yes, you would have done as you suggested."

"So what do you think the outcome will be if we don't settle?"

"The court is likely to order the three bars held in Ms. Falk's name to be sold, all attorney fees and court costs paid, her final expenses be paid and the remaining proceeds divided four ways."

A horrible taste invaded my mouth. I shook with rage. Taking a few deep breaths first to try and calm down, I finally leveled him with my gaze. "Those people have been no part whatsoever of Lisa's life for nearly twenty years. It's my own fault, I know; had I not told them she passed, we wouldn't even be here. I'll be damned if I'm going to just hand them 3/4ths of her estate, her life's work!"

"If we don't settle, you won't have a choice."

"You're certain?"

"As I can be. I told you once before, we're not in the odds laying business but precedents have been established in the courts that point toward the sort of outcome I've given you."

Sighing, I resigned myself to what appeared to be inevitable, "What sort of deal are you recommending we make?"

"Your home and the business in Steamboat are yours, free and clear under joint tenancy. We don't even put those on the table. We stipulate that all of Ms. Falk's personal assets – her car, her IRA – roll over to you."

"Those vultures don't want those things anyway. They're in this for a big cash windfall. The money is in the businesses."

"Right," he nodded. "So, we propose that you keep one of the three bars and liquidate the other two. I would suggest selling the two you think would be the easiest to move in the current business climate. The resulting monies would be split between the three plaintiffs minus court costs and their attorney fees. They would agree to have no further claim on Ms. Falk's estate."

"What about Lisa's bills and your fees?"

He leaned back and pursed his lips.

"So those are on me?"

Chapter 7

Tuesday, July 16th, 2013
Owl Title Company
Steamboat Springs, Colorado

"I just want to move on with my life and be allowed to grieve for Lisa. I can't do that with so much debt hanging over my head."

Cross stared at me for a minute but I didn't back down. "Let's go in then and get this deal done, then," he finally said.

Kane, Roger and the male title agent rose as we entered the conference room but I waved them back into their seats.

"Ma'am, gentlemen," Cross began to address all of those assembled in the room before we were even seated.

I put a hand on his arm to draw his focus back to me and, once I had it, I told him, "I've got this."

Nodding to my two friends Kane and Roger and to the woman, presumably their lawyer, seated to Kane's right, I jumped right in, "So, you want to buy Willie's and I want to sell it. I think we're all in agreement on that, right?" There were nods and smiles all around. "I've seen your offer," I continued, looking again at my two friends, "and it's very fair. Sold!"

An even broader grin spread across Kane's face. I smiled then too. "These folks have lots of details to hash out and paperwork to churn up before we can all sign on the dotted line," I said as I waggled a finger at the two lawyers and the title agent. What do you say we leave them to it and go grab a bite, my treat?"

"Sounds good," Roger said rising.

"I'm real sorry you feel like you had to sell the place Barb, but I have to say, I never thought buying a business would be quite so easy."

Roger sputtered on a mouthful of coffee and I laughed at Kane's naivety.

"What? It is easy." Kane said again as he looked back and forth between the two of us.

"Buying it may be...but just wait till we're back in that conference room and you feel like you're signing your life away," I told him. "And then there's the day to day running of the place once it's legally yours."

Recovering enough to speak, Roger choked out, "He has no idea."

"That's where you come in Uncle Rog." Kane smiled at the older man.

"Oh, you got that right, but I'm going to teach you everything I know about managing an establishment and then I'm going to take a backseat and live off my half of the profits."

I chuckled at that too. For the first time in weeks, my burden felt a little lighter and my grief just a little less palpable.

"It's good to see you smile," Roger said to me.

I tipped my head toward him. "It's been rough; I'm not going to lie. I'm really missing Lisa and...Listen; I really appreciate everything you two have done. You've kept things going, you've kept me going..."

Roger picked up the hand I was waving about. "That's what friends are for," he said simply.

"I still feel kind of bad about all of this, though," Kane put in again.

"Don't, okay? What you didn't know is Lisa and I were grooming you to manage the bar anyway. Our plans were to sell Willie's and move on once we were sure you could impress a new owner enough to keep you on. That you're one of the new owners is even better. I have a lot less heartburn about this deal than I have about a couple of others we've made in the past."

"Less? There is some then?" he asked me back.

"There's always some. Willie's is a good bar, good crowd – local and tourist. It's bittersweet letting go of it and even more so since it was the last..." I got chocked up and took several seconds to compose myself while the server delivered our orders.

"Pardon my nosy curiosity," Roger excused himself, "but what are your plans now? I mean, I know your other businesses are still caught up in probate."

"It's okay. I really can't go anywhere until all of that's resolved and, frankly, I don't know that

I want to continue on without Lisa. I just wanted to get her bills paid and have a little money to live on while everything else is tied up in court."

"I appreciate all you've done for me Barb and all you've taught me," Kane spoke up. "I hope you don't mind me...us...picking your brain from time to time." He looked at his uncle for his confirming nodded.

"Of course and, it's actually in the agreement. I want you to succeed."

"So you'll come around from time to time?"

"Count on it."

"Good, good," Roger said. "You're welcome by any time...you're just one of the guys...so to speak."

Thursday Evening, August 15th, 2013
Steamboat Willie's

"Barb's here again?" Roger asked Kane.

The younger man nodded. "Drowning her sorrows for the third night this week."

"I love her to death," Roger said shaking his head, "but she really dampens the vibe of the place. She needs something else to do."

"She's still grieving...I hate to say anything..." Kane shrugged and moved toward a beckoning customer.

Roger went the other way, toward Barb. "Hey, how ya doing?" he asked the sullen woman when he reached her corner of the bar.

"I'm fine. Celebrating." Barb took a sip of her drink.

"Celebrating? What?" His tone was curious but cautious.

"The deal was approved by the courts yesterday to sell the bars and there was already a good offer pending on one of them because I put the word out a few weeks ago that it might be coming available."

"Barb, that's great! I mean, I know you didn't really want to have to give up anything at all but..."

"No but you're right. It's a good thing." She took a deep breath and let it out slowly. Looking down, she studied the drink her hand was curved around. "Maybe now I can work on moving on."

"It's early yet, honey; you're entitled to grieve, you know?" Roger looked at her glass himself and decided to change the subject back to her small victory of the day. "How about a little dinner celebration over the agreement, you and me, on Kane?"

Barb smiled at that but before she could offer a reply, Roger added, "We got in some of the best honey glazed turkey today I've ever had, some California avocado...it'll all make some killer sandwiches."

"I know what you're doing my friend but it does sound good."

Roger held back a smile as she looked down again and pushed the half-finished drink toward him. He took the glass and, over his shoulder as he headed toward the kitchen, he said, "Coming right up."

"Hey pretty lady, how are you?"

I looked to my right as a man slid onto the bar stool beside me. "Stephen, what a nice surprise! I haven't seen you since...since..."

"The funeral, I know and I'm sorry about that," He finished my thought for me. "In my defense, it's been crazy busy at work. I've been picking up all of the extra shifts I can handle."

I winced. "You better be careful or you're going to burn out."

He half shrugged. "It's all good. We're working on a plan to expand the facilities and offer more services. It's tough on the locals and all the tourists when anything more than a basic sprain or break or something more serious has to be referred to Denver, you know?"

I dropped my head.

Stephen caught on quick. "Barb, I'm sorry...I...that was insensitive."

Putting my hand on his arm and marshalling a little inner strength, I told him, "I'm working on moving on. I need to. It's been pointed out to me – subtly – that drinking myself to death isn't a good option." As if on cue,

Roger reappeared bearing two plates and tipped his head toward an empty floor table.

"There's my dinner and, by the looks of that sandwich, it's enough for four. Join us?"

"Don't mind if I do but not to eat. I grabbed a bite before I went off shift. Talking to you has reminded me though; I have something to tell you that you might be interested in...if, that is, you don't mind chatting in front of Roger?"

"There's no real way to sugarcoat this so I'm just going to get right to the point," Stephen looked to me for confirmation. I gave him a slight nod to tell him he should continue.

"The surgeon at Denver General, Simmons, who performed Lisa's operation, was called before the medical review board. He lost his license to practice."

I nearly dropped the half sub I was holding. "What? Are you sure?"

Stephen nodded. "Positive. It's all over the med center. Several of the docs have referred cancer patients to him. They're all talking."

"Why? Do you know?"

"I saw something on the news," Roger interjected, "but I didn't put two and two together." He shook his head slowly. "Malpractice? I think that's what they were implying."

"The official party line is 'Unsafe Acts'. I'm here to tell you it has to go a whole lot deeper than that to yank someone's license to practice medicine."

"What does that have to do with me; with Lisa? They know a blood clot killed her."

"That's just it Barb, what if it could have been prevented? What if Simmons didn't do something he was supposed to do or didn't do something...I don't know...didn't do something correctly? Her death was tragic. Could it have been needless too?"

"You're saying I should ask for some sort of investigation?"

"That's up to you but, if it was me and my partner, either one of us would be talking to a lawyer, wanting some answers."

I turned my nose up. "Not again. No more lawyers. I'm sick of dealing with people that only want the easy way to a big payday for them."

"Barb," Roger said, reaching for my hand, "it might bear looking into. Look what you've lost in terms of medical costs alone for Lisa. If they find something and you sue the hospital for wrongful death..." He trailed off. The three of us sat there and stared at each other for a good minute.

Chapter 8

Monday, February 17th, 2014
Denver, Colorado

I tugged my blue suit out of the plastic bag the dry cleaner had covered it with. It was the only nice thing I owned that didn't reek of cigarette smoke from the private club I'd been tending bar at to make ends meet.

My black pumps were missing in action. It took me all of thirty seconds to do a swing around the tiny apartment I'd been living in for the past four and a half months to find them. Slipping them on as I stood in front of the mirror on the back of the only door into the place, I shook my head at myself.

"It will have to do," I said out loud to the barren walls. I grabbed my little satchel of papers off the wood breakfast table that had been left behind by the previous occupant, collected my keys and locked my way out with a scant backward glance into the depressing rooms I hoped I wouldn't be occupying much longer.

It felt like it took forever to find a parking space in downtown Denver, near the Common Pleas Court Complex. Now a few minutes late, once I was through security, I rushed to find my floor and my lawyer.

My cell was buzzing as I stepped off the elevator. Before I could dig it out, I spied Rufus James rushing toward me as he pocketed his own phone. "Barb," he called out, "this way." He motioned for me to follow him.

"Sorry I'm late," I said as I stepped through the doorway of the small conference room he'd gone into.

"You're fine. The judge just took the dais and there's a hearing ahead of ours. But what's more pressing here is that I was right, Barb."

I tipped my head sideways and studied the well dressed, middle aged black man in front of me. "About?" I was confused.

"When word leaked about this lawsuit, and might I remind you, I had nothing whatsoever to do with that," he waggled a finger, "others started jumping on the band wagon. They want to sweep us under the rug. They don't even want this pre-lim to take place today."

"Sweep us under the rug how?"

"Settlement. They want to settle."

"Been there, done that Rufus. I told you that. It didn't go well for me. Just to pay off the rest of what was owed after my last go around with the Colorado court system and make sure I could cover your fees if things went south for me here, I sold off the home I owned in Steamboat and the last bar I still owned. All my worldly possessions that don't fit in the crappy little apartment I'm living in right now are in storage.

'Settlement'," I made air quotes, "doesn't sound very appealing."

I leaned back in the chair I'd sunk into and thought for a minute. Wisely, he let me think, uninterrupted.

Finally, I asked him, "Where's *your* head at with this turn?"

He spoke carefully and laid out his thinking. "We got a copy of the Coroner's report three months ago. No Heparin in Lisa's system. Her charts bear that out. Simmons never ordered it. Additionally, she was made to wait while another surgery moved ahead of hers. Those events combined to create the clot that killed her."

He paused and turned his body toward me from his seat adjacent to me at one end of the conference table. Leaning toward me and speaking low, he told me, "We have them nailed Barb. They don't know what all is coming down the pipe but they know there was negligence all the way around here, with this case. They want to settle with you so they can get this case gone – quietly – and they can gird themselves for the rest of the battles they'll be facing."

"How does that help me? I mean, if we have them nailed, as you put it, wouldn't we do better going to a jury trial?"

Before he could answer, I held a hand up to stop him. "Dumb question. Forget I asked it. Now, listen to me," I said. "It's not about the money. It's never been about the money..."

Now Rufus held a hand up. "Barb, dear, it's *always* about the money. You've lost Lisa and, in the process of dealing with your loss, you've lost a great deal of your life's work and paid out for things that you never should have paid out for had Denver General not been completely negligent. "You tell me. You decide. Do we invite their team in here and try and hash out a deal or do we proceed with today's hearing, as planned? I'm with you for the duration, either way."

"If we can't come to some sort of agreement with them, what are our chances of getting another hearing scheduled before the dam bursts with a flood of new cases?"

"The docket is full for the next month plus, but that means those other cases will be waiting too. We're in the driver's seat. We don't have a lot to lose by either settling or by being first."

I twisted up my face and drummed my fingers on the table top as I thought about the two options. Letting out a small sigh, I told Rufus, "I'm just not real confident that I'm not going to get screwed over again."

"I'm not going to let that happen Barb. We don't like their offer, we walk and we let a jury dictate what they pay. My job is to get you the best deal I can."

"And yourself."

He nodded. "Precisely. I haven't been in business this long by not doing right by people."

"Okay. Get them in here."

Broken Women

48

Chapter 9

I was dumbfounded as I sat scribbling on a notepad while my lawyer and the team of three lawyers from Denver General bickered back and forth. The total of Lisa's medical bills, for a botched surgery, came to well over $700,000, some that our insurance paid and a lot that I paid. If Rufus got his way – and it was starting to look like he might – all of it would be repaid apart from any other award. That alone made me feel more at ease.

Keeping to myself, even though I was seated right in the thick of things, I just listened as they carried on. True to his word, Rufus was my steady advocate. He looked to his left at me for confirmation frequently but I just nodded and kept my face as unreadable as I could otherwise. I certainly didn't want to give anything away and I didn't want to get my hopes up too high either.

After a bit of listening to their negotiating, my mind started to wander, going back over what had brought me to this point. It had been a tough stretch for me since that last night at Willie's. Stephen and Roger and later even Kane joined in on prodding me to sue. I wasn't as sure as they all were but, after a couple of days of thought, I decided they were right.

Stephen telling me Simmons had lost his license to practice had opened a fresh hole in my wounded heart and the pain was nearly unbearable as I contemplated over the next 48

49

hours whether he'd been directly responsible for Lisa's death. I felt like I needed to find out for sure.

Our usual law firm wouldn't take the case on. They weren't 'tort lawyers', they told me. They referred me to a firm in Denver that turned out to be little more than an ambulance chasing operation; not at all what I wanted.

The Bar Association gave me Rufus James' name, along with a couple of others. I looked them all up. Rufus was the best. He was also the most expensive on an hour by hour basis. If we didn't win, I was going to owe him the moon. That's why I'd sold everything I had remaining. Now, that was dwindling away too as the last of the medical bills had rolled in and other expenses, like costs for selling my home, popped up.

I wasn't necessarily sorry to let the house go. We...I...hadn't even been there a year. With Willie's sold, I had no ties at all to Steamboat. Unfortunately, there was little equity there either. The small gain the market had made during the time we owned the beautiful house was more than negated by the cost of listing the place for sale and then closing the deal.

Moving the three-hour drive to Denver to be closer to everything seemed like a smart move at the time. I took the cheapest place I could find that was close to center city. When all the preliminary wrangling for discovery and such went on and on with no end in sight, I took the job at the club just to get myself out of the apartment and earning some money rather than spending everything that I'd set aside. The job didn't help me stop thinking about Lisa but it dulled the pain just a little while I was on duty.

Without thinking, I shook my head. Rufus paused in his patter and looked at me. "Sorry. You were saying?" I said to him.

He continued laying out a case for a 'Pain and Suffering' award by ticking off the points of my distress on his fingers. I tuned him out again, on purpose this time. Outside of work, where I had no other distractions, my pain was still very raw and every one of these types of meetings made it that much sharper.

"Let me confer privately with my client," Rufus was saying, several minutes into my reverie. I simply nodded. I'd been so lost in my own thoughts; I wasn't quite sure where things stood.

He indicated we should step out of the little conference room. "Gentlemen, give us about twenty minutes or so to go over these numbers." There were murmurs of agreement from the other side as he collected up all of his papers and then we were moving into the hallway.

"Coffee?" he asked me once we were out of earshot of the conference room.

"Sounds good."

The elevator was full. We stayed silent as we rode down to the cafeteria. I felt bad that I'd been so out of it, I didn't even know what sort of deal we were about to discuss but I had the strange feeling Rufus already knew that.

We got coffee and took seats at a corner table in the mostly empty cafeteria. It wasn't time for the lunch rush yet. He popped his briefcase back open, took his pad out and turned it to face me.

Tapping some figures with his pen, he said, "They'll cover all medical bills. We have an accounting from the insurance company of everything that passed through them, the claims they paid and the amounts that were not covered. We have copies of all of the bills you received, your canceled checks, the statements and so forth. All of that, every cent, to be reimbursed, one for one. It comes to $757,000 and change. Nearly $300,000 of that goes to you."

I nodded. "And you get a part of that, right?"

He shook his head, "Not a dime, not a dime. That's all reimbursement and pretty standard in medical negligence cases. I wouldn't have it any other way."

Rufus sipped his coffee before continuing. He pointed back at the paper as he told me, "the State of Colorado" limits compensatory damage awards and pain and suffering awards that can be granted by a jury. We've talked about that."

"Yes."

"There are no such limitations on private settlements. In exchange for this being settled out of court and for you signing a non-disclosure agreement barring you from ever talking about the settlement, they're offering $1,890,000; roughly two and a half times the medical claims."

I nearly spilled my coffee, catching it only as it was almost completely toppled. A little of the hot liquid sloshed out of the lidded cup onto my hand. I felt the sting but, after the catch, I was rendered nearly oblivious to it. The liquid dripped off onto the table edge and down to my slacks as I put my hand to my mouth.

Rufus quickly handed me a napkin but was otherwise patient. He let me absorb what he'd just told me for several long minutes.

When I finally found the ability to speak again, I asked him, my voice shaking, "Could you break that down for me please. I'm...I'm trying to get my head around it..."

"It works out to just over $297,000 for the medical bills that you've paid out of pocket and about a million, two-fifty or a little more after my fees and court costs for the pain and suffering award they're proposing."

I just let the tears fall.

Friday, March 14th, 2014

Denver was in my rearview mirror by 5:00 AM on a mid-March Friday morning. Once everything was settled with the hospital, there wasn't a reason in the world for me to stay there. I couldn't stay there. I just couldn't.

I'd packed up the personal belongings I knew I'd need over the next couple of weeks, picked up Lisa's urn and got on I-70. I drove it all the way to Zanesville over the next couple of days.

My parents were happy to have me back in town. I never thought I'd be there long term again but then, they're all I have left in the world now.

Part Two

Janet

Chapter 10

Janet Mason

April 23rd, 2008, Somewhere in the Middle East

"What took you so long, Mason?"

"Top wouldn't shut up. I swear that man likes to hear himself speak."

Kyra tugged me into a curtained off shower stall. "Get that gear off. We don't have a lot of time before the privates take over." She was already naked herself and wet in more ways than one.

"Yes ma'am!"

"That's Sergeant to you, Corporal," she ordered, her tone only half official.

"Yes Sergeant!" I responded enthusiastically.

I dropped my flak jacket and web gear on the little bench just outside the stall and bent to unlace my boots. Kyra took my flipped over state as an opportunity to hump my still camo clad ass.

"My favorite Sergeant is a horny toad today," I called up to her.

"Who you calling a toad? You'll pay for that!"

"Oh, I don't think so, Sarge."

Quickly, I stripped out of the rest of my uniform and my skivvies while Kyra restarted the water flow.

Moving in behind her, I embraced her and started teasing her nipples with my fingers. I was determined to give her a ride this time she wouldn't forget. Knowing she was already wet, while one set of fingers worked a nipple, I dropped the other hand to her pussy and ran my fingers through her shower dampened curls to her slit. It too was slick with moist heat, this from her core.

Kyra arched her ass into my own center and ground herself against me. I groaned in both pleasure and pain but I was determined to stay focused and give the butch beauty as good a fuck as she'd given me days before.

My own breasts tingled against her back as she bucked and tried to mount my fingers. "The tables are turned Sarge," I said as I dipped my head and bit her gently at the curve of her neck.

"No marks Mason!"

"No marks, Sarge; just a hard fuck." I pulled her tight back into me and pushed two fingers as deep as I could into her swollen center.

She was dripping with her own juices. "Somebody started the party without me," I said into her neck as I moved my fingers in and out.

"Told you we don't have a lot of time," she panted.

Taking the hint, I quickened the pace and watched over her shoulder as she bit down on her bottom lip to keep from crying out. Moments later, she came in a sticky burst. I thumbed her clit as I continued to stroke her slit with my other fingers and she orgasmed again in a shudder.

"Your turn," she said as she tried to turn into me on shaky legs.

"Nope," I said. "Not this time."

"Hey, I'm supposed to be the aggressor here..."

"We don't have a lot of time; you said it yourself and, anyway, Happy Birthday."

"So that's what this was all about?"

"My gift to you."

"Well now how will I ever thank you?" She lifted her eyebrows suggestively.

"Oh, I don't know. I'm sure you'll think of something demeaning and degrading." I grinned to show my pleasure at the thought of another lovemaking session with her and I tried to lean in for a kiss.

Kyra backed off. "We need to get dressed," she said hurriedly.

Figuring she was just nervous about being caught when NCO time in the shower bay was up and the free-for-all of privates and specialists descended upon the makeshift building in the middle of nowhere, I didn't really make anything of her withdrawal or the change in her tone. Instead, I asked, "Since it's your birthday and all, do you wanna, I don't know, hang out tonight? Play cards or something?"

"You can buy me a birthday Coke at the Den, Mason."

Chapter 11

'The Den' as 'The Devil Dogs Den' was called for short, to appease local sensibilities, was slammed. I scanned the crowd looking for Kyra and spotted her holding court with some of the other female NCOs in the unit at a little table off to one side of the makeshift tent turned clubhouse.

"A Coke and a diet, please," I told the sergeant taking orders at the counter. I took the drinks and weaved my way through the throngs of soldiers crowded in for lack of any other place to go and hang out when they were off duty.

"Hey," I nodded in greeting to the five women gathered around the table. Most of them nodded back at me.

I handed the Coke to Kyra. "Happy Birthday Sarge."

"Thank you Corporal Mason. That's very nice of you."

So we're being formal now. Okay. I can do this. While I composed my face, I swiveled looking for an empty chair to grab and managed to swipe one from a couple of tables over just before a Private attempted to commandeer it for himself.

As I set it down at our table, one of the other Sergeants present, Gevona Moore, waggled a finger at me. "Now I owe her Mason, thanks to you. I didn't get her anything."

"As if there's much to get out here in the desert," one of the other women snickered.

"Oh that?" I played it off. "It's nothing. I owed her that myself."

Gevona looked at Kyra. "Girl, I'm broke till payday but you know I got you. Hit me up next week and, well hell, it'll be Cokes all around." She bobbed her head to indicate all of us at the table.

"Mm, Mm, why so generous, throwing three bucks around, Moore?" Kyra asked her. Everyone laughed.

"Hey, you all know I've been sending most of my money home these last couple of months. I need a security deposit, first month's rent, utility deposits..."

"Why? You aren't going anywhere," Kyra chided her.

"The hell I ain't," she retorted, in a slightly lowered voice.

"You're not going to re-up and do another tour to hang out here with all of us?" another woman asked.

"No ma'am, not me. I only took the tour extension I did because the commander agreed to let me halve it. At my liberty break next month, I'm going back stateside and staying. I ETS out in 62 days."

"What are you in such a hurry to get back to – Indiana is it? – for?" Kyra put in.

Gevona leveled her coal black eyes on Kyra. "I didn't join the Army for it to be a career. You know that." Kyra shrugged but held her gaze. "I never said that, not once," she continued.

"What will you do when you ETS?" I asked her.

"For one, I want to be a real cop, not an MP that gets sent off to pull duty in Godforsaken places like this place for months on end."

"What else Moore?" Kyra prodded her. Gevona just looked at her.

Kyra wouldn't let it go. "You said, 'for one'. There must be something else, right?"

Deep down, I thought I knew what the something else was. I was pretty sure the caramel skinned beauty played for the same team as Kyra and I did but, if she had any interest in any of the women in the unit, she was very discreet about it.

"Look, I just want to be a cop when I'm on duty and a civilian free to live my life, my way when I'm off, that's all. I'm tired of playing by military rules 24/7."

Well that confirms it for me.

I almost choked on my Diet Coke when the conversation suddenly turned my way. Sargent Cami Streit, who was the unit admin and who'd been quiet to that point, focused on me. "Isn't your ETS coming up quick too, Mason?"

"Yeah, in a coupla months."

"You re-upping?" she quizzed me. Kyra and Gevona both watched me closely.

Under the scrutiny of everyone at the table, I felt myself waver a little bit but I bucked up and

told them what was really going through my
head. "The only reason I joined was because I
was too young to go to OPOTA, the Ohio Peace
Officer's Training Academy course, when I got
out of school. All I really want to do is to be a
cop too."

"So, you're getting out?" Gevona asked me.

I looked at her and then at Kyra who was
now feigning interest in the nearest support post
holding up the tent wall. I could almost feel her
disinterest. "I'm not sure. Probably."

Chapter 12

April 24th, 2008

"Kyra's a player. You ain't gonna' change that."

Gevona and I were talking quietly while we waited out by the Hummer for the Private that was assigned to be our M60 gunner to draw his ammo for convoy escort duty.

I just looked at her and didn't say anything.

"You wanna be a cop, right?"

I nodded.

"Where you going back to? Ohio, you said?" She leaned back against the vehicle.

"Don't know...that's my problem. I want to get out and get on a force somewhere but I don't want to go back to frick'en Zanesville, Ohio."

"That where your family is?"

"Yeah. And they're okay...sorta. My mom and I don't really see eye to eye and...there's nothing there for me, you know?" I shot her a look. She gave me a slight nod in return.

"I grew up on the west side of Indy. I'm not in an all fired hurry to get back there either but anywhere in Indy is better than anywhere in the Army right now, if you know what I mean." She didn't look me in the eye but stared straight ahead watching the supply line for the progress of the Private.

"Did you apply somewhere there already?"

Turning back to me at that, she said, "Just between you and me – not that anyone else here really cares – but I'm applying to be a deputy with Hancock County, just east of Marion County."

"That near Indy?"

"Yeah, Indy takes up most of Marion County."

"Why there? Why not the Indy city department?"

"Because it'll be a lot easier to get on and I can still live and play in the city. Hancock's actively hiring women right now. They're busy and they need to get their quota up. I fit the requirements on two counts and, with my MP experience..." She shrugged.

"Why do you say they're busy?"

"They're right on the I-70 corridor that runs through the state. Lotta' drug trade moves through on the way into the city and on to St. Louis."

"Wow." I was dumbfounded. "Funny, I grew up right off of 70 in Zanesville. I guess I just hadn't thought of it like that."

"Oh yeah, girl. Hancock needs all the help they can get trying to stem that tide."

"Do you think they'd hire me...I mean if it's okay with you..." I stopped talking, unsure of myself.

"It ain't up to me but I just told you; They need help and they need more women. You're not black but you're female and you have law enforcement training."

"I...I just don't want to step on your toes or anything. It's your thing and..."

"Listen, Mason," she interrupted, "I wouldn't be telling you about it if I wanted to keep it some big secret. And, just so you know, I'm going to be looking for a roommate to split costs with, at least for a little while. Would you be interested in that?"

Chapter 13

Late Friday Evening, June 24th, 2011
Greenfield Indiana

"Me and some of the girls are going to The Underground after we bust outa' here tonight; you in?"

I stopped working on an arrest report and looked at her. "That new dance club up in Broad Ripple?" I set my mouth in a grim line. I'm not much of a dancer.

Gevona caught my look and gave me her best pouty face. "Come on; we finally got a back to back, Friday, Saturday night off."

"Technically, we're working. This is Friday."

"Whatever Mason!" She swung a hand at me. "You know what I mean. We can dance all night because we don't have to be back here tomorrow night. It'll be fun."

"I didn't bring *nice* clothes with me tonight." I tried to make an excuse.

"No prob! Our apartment's on the way. We can stop real quick. Wear that blue blouse your mom sent you for your birthday. You look nice in that."

It took all I had to control a smile. I hadn't thought she paid much attention to me like that.

"Are you in or not?"

I let out a fake sigh. "I suppose."

"Good; that makes six of us then. You and me will ride together and meet up with the others." She nudged me with an elbow, "Who knows, you may just get lucky tonight." I choked back the lump that rose in my throat while she continued with her train of thought, "We're gonna' find you a lady friend. You've been all about the job ever since we got out of the Army."

12:05 AM, Saturday Morning, June 25th, 2011
The Underground

The old bar turned alternative dance club was jumping when we finally got there just after midnight.

I looked at Gevona. She was an absolute knockout in a red dress she'd decided to 'slip into' since we had to stop by the apartment for me to change anyway. She'd primped her makeup in the locker room beforehand and slipped into jeans there that I'd thought she looked just as good in but, either way, I wasn't complaining.

"This is unreal," she yelled to me as we finally squeezed our way past the front door security.

The music was loud and thumping. Guys were grinding with other guys and women were all over each other on the crowded dance floor positioned straight out in front of us. Beyond them was the raised DJ booth where a shirtless guy was spinning. A small stage, presumably for a band, stood next to his booth but it wasn't empty, even though he was playing. Bolder club patrons were up there putting on a show while pretending to be oblivious to those looking on.

"We'll never find our crew in here," I called out to Gevona as I scanned the crowd thronged to the left of the dance floor. Some were watching the floor while others had their backs to it, vying for drinks at the bar that ran almost the length of the left wall. Half a dozen male and female bartenders worked the crowd, the males shirtless and the women only barely covered.

"Girl, they're probably already dancing!" she called back. "Oh wait," she paused and started again, "I think that's Bennie over there." She pointed off to the right of the dance floor somewhere where there was more floor space that was mostly taken up by a full square bar more toward the front of the club with small tables behind that.

I couldn't pick Bonita Harris, 'Bennie' as she preferred to be called, out of the teeming crowd on that side of the room but Gevona headed that way and I followed.

We weaved our way in and out and around people as we worked our way past the bar and toward a raised platform of sofa like seating and tables along the right side wall. *They've got to be way over their fire capacity limits in here...*

My thoughts were interrupted by Gevona grabbing my arm. She pointed with her other hand then waved as she leaned in to me and said, "It is Bennie, see?"

The other woman was waving back at us from a seat on one of the couches. As we continued toward her, the other three women from the department all arrived at the couch from an area somewhere ahead of us. Slightly annoyed, I shook my head. I suspected they'd been on a mass bathroom trip. *What makes completely capable police officers act like school girls in a place like this?*

Gevona waggled her head at the group as we finally got through the throngs and reached the roped off and elevated area. "VIP seating ladies? What gives?"

"With bottle service," Bennie replied, indicating the Vodka, mixers and ice already on the little table. "It cost a little bit more but I, uh, know one of the bartenders so I got a little break." She raised her eyebrows suggestively.

"I'm in," Gevona told her. "What's my cut?"

"Just $50 right now, with tip. If we get another bottle..."

"It's okay," Gevona said as she turned to me. "What about you Janet?"

Not knowing what else to say and not wanting to be a party pooper, I said, "Count me in too but, I'm not really a vodka drinker." I took out my wallet when I could see my roommate doing the same and we both handed Bennie our share.

"They'll bring you something else Janet," Bennie told me. "It's just, if you get a whole bottle, it's more."

"It's okay; I'll make do." Somebody should be the designated driver anyway, I thought to myself. It wouldn't do to have any of our deputies picked up for a DUI.

A woman came by dressed in next to nothing and, within seconds, was fixing Gevona a drink. After Bennie pressed a little money in her hand – presumably some of what we'd just turned over to her – I caught her attention myself.

As she leaned over to me where I sat, her boobs prominently displayed right in front of me, I smiled but managed to pull my focus up to her face. "I'm the driver for this bunch. Can you get me a soda water with orange and cranberry?" I asked her, while trying not to be overheard. It wasn't hard in the din of the place.

"Sure thing sweetie. Nothing else?"

I just shook my head no.

Gevona was gyrating on the floor with some very tall black woman who, I wasn't entirely sure but I strongly suspected, was a male to female transgender woman. I'd catch occasional flashes of her red dress or her grinning face as the two of them put on quite a show.

I'd found a spot at the rail along the floor where I was slowly sipping my juice mixer and watching the crowd. I'd left the safety of the banquette of sofas when the other ladies started pairing off with women from the club. It was getting a little too 'couples oriented' back there behind me for my tastes.

Someone squeezed in beside me. I turned to find a tall, blue eyed, butch woman looking down at me. I'm not short, but she had me by several inches. She smiled and leaned back a little so I didn't have to look into her neck.

"You're not dancing?"

"Not much of a dancer," I smiled back at her, opting for being polite and friendly.

"Can I buy you another drink?" she asked me as she pointed at my glass that was now only about a third full.

"Sorry, it's just juice." I held the glass up, "Designated driver; I'm here with friends."

She smiled again. "I'm trying everything here. I usually don't have to work this hard."

We'd been talking less than 10 seconds but, deciding to cut her a break, I offered her my hand. "I'm Janet. And you are?"

She never got a chance to respond. A ruckus arose from behind me and, instinctually, I turned toward it.

A rather large, beefy male, presumably a customer given his position on the outside of the square bar, had another man, a manager I suspected, given his shirt and tie and position on the inside of the bar, in a headlock. Even from my vantage point several feet away, it was obvious the manager was choking for air. His face was turning a growing shade of red as he struggled against the other man's hold.

Drawing my badge wallet out, I bolted for them as I yelled "Sheriff's Deputy!" The crowd between the rail and the bar parted and let me pass.

I was out of my jurisdiction but assault is assault and I wasn't going to let the situation get any further. I got right up to the two men and ordered the aggressor to stand down and stay right where he was. He released his chokehold on the other man but he kept a hold of his arm.

"Let him go now," I ordered.

The security guy I remembered from the front door appeared behind him and did some sort of move on him I couldn't see from my viewpoint that got him in his control and caused him to release the other man from his grip.

I looked around the tall man at the bouncer. "Is there somewhere we can take these two?"

He pointed toward the back of the club.

"Let's go, all of you," I told them in my no-nonsense voice.

A young woman, likely barely 21, that I hadn't noticed before, stepped from the outside of the bar on the other side of the aggressor. Her face was tear stained, mascara running from her eyes in a spiderlike effect that she'd smudged as she dabbed at it. She followed behind us, whimpering.

At his reluctance, I prompted the manager to leave the relative safety of the bar and go with us and put a hand on him to propel him forward when he was still reluctant to move. We followed behind the security guy who kept a firm grasp on the customer as we headed toward a hallway off the back, to the right of the stage.

A security guard back there stood when we approached but let the bouncer and his charge pass into the hallway without question. "Sheriff's department," I called to him from behind the man I was loosely escorting. Turning, I saw the younger woman was still following us. "She's with us too."

He was keying his mike as I stepped past and I heard him call, "Barb, security office."

The bouncer led us all into a room with a desk and chair and two additional chairs. It was small and cramped and otherwise unadorned. He directed his charge to one chair. The girl followed and stood next to him. The guy from the hallway tried to squeeze in too.

Thinking better of sitting the manager next to his aggressor, I directed him to a corner behind the desk then I took charge. Looking at the guy in the shirt and tie, I asked him, "I assume you work here?"

He nodded.

"And your name is?"

"Geoff."

"I'm not here to play games. Geoff, what?"

"Jamison. I'm one of the assistant managers."

"You're a damn rapist is what you are!" the other man spat at him. I put out a hand to quiet him.

The door, which was only partially closed given the crowd already jammed into the small room, swung in a little. A woman I estimated to be about five or six years older than me with short blond hair stepped in and eyed the scene.

"And you are?" I asked her next.

"Barbara, uh, Falk. I'm one of the owners. What's going on?"

"These two, I pointed at her manager and the other man, had a little tussle out there at the bar. I'm with the Sheriff's Department. I'm just trying to get to the bottom of it."

"I'll tell you what happened," the aggressor piped up again. "Your manager over here tried to rape my sister." He looked at the young woman standing next to him. She hung her head.

"Is this true?" Falk questioned Geoff.

"I ain't talkin' in front of all of these people," was all he would say in reply.

Angry didn't begin to describe the way I was feeling. "We need to get this figured out and I'm not leaving until we do." I turned to the owner, "Ma'am, you should stay. I can handle this. If you want to send your security team back out to their posts?"

She nodded and directed the two men back to work then closed the door behind them and leaned against it.

"Okay, you are?" I asked the man who'd started the fight.

"Michael Walls. This is my younger sister Katie." He looked at Falk as he continued, "I come in here every once in a while." She nodded in support of his claim. Seeing that, he went on. "Katie's just coming out. I admit, I haven't been the best big brother but...I was just trying to help her loosen up a little and then this...this scumbag..." He flung a hand toward Geoff Jamison.

"Mike don't; it's okay. Let's just go," she told him softly.

The sound of her plea, as quiet as it was, reverberated in the tiny room. My heart went out to her.

"It's not okay," he told his sister.

"Katie, can you tell us what happened?" I asked her in the gentlest tone I could muster.

She wouldn't look up at me. I knew I needed to separate her from the two men and interview her separately but I was stuck between a rock and a hard place. That's when I remembered my friends.

"Ms. Falk, do you have an office back here?"

"Just down the hall."

"Would you take Katie back there please and also ask the security guard at the end of this hallway to have the DJ page a Gevona and a Bennie to come back here please? They're deputies too."

Barbara moved forward, took the younger girls hand and led her from the room without another word.

I waited in the small office the three or four minutes it took for first Gevona and then Bennie to show up. They both looked somewhat shocked at seeing me back there but quickly moved professional masks into place as I told them what I knew to that point.

"I'm going to step over to the owner's office and get a statement from the alleged victim," I whispered to them, hopefully out of the earshot of her still incensed brother. "I'll call Marion County from there. See what you can get from these two."

Barbara Falk graciously handed her office over to me when I explained to her that I wanted to interview Katie privately. I stepped outside the office with her briefly first and admitted to her that I was actually with Hancock County and would be calling Marion County in. She thanked me for my honesty and moved off to see what Bennie and Gevona had dredged up with her manager and her customer.

It was a very long night after that as the Marion Department didn't send a female officer over and Katie wouldn't talk about what happened to either of the men that did show up. I was the only one she would open up to.

When she was reunited with her brother, he convinced her to press charges against the manager for assault, at a minimum. I felt like, after talking with her and after hearing what little Geoff had to say in his own defense, he should have been charged with attempted rape too but that was between the victim and Marion County. Once they had her statement, I was effectively out of it, at least for the time being.

After turning a night out on the town into a case, I took no small amount of flak from my fellow deputy and roommate for always being on the job.

Chapter 14

*Saturday Night, 11:20 PM December 31ˢᵗ, 2011
Greenfield, Indiana*

"I actually thought we'd be busier."

Shrugging, I replied to Gevona, "The mid shift probably will be once all the clubs and bars ring in the New Year and then close up."

We climbed into her little car and she steered us out of the parking lot. I wasn't sure how to broach the subject with her but, finally, trying to keep my tone neutral, I just asked her; "Are you going out with Lexi tonight?"

I feared the answer but I had to know. She'd been hot and heavy with the voluptuous brunette for a couple of weeks and had spent little of our off duty time at home. She was always with the other woman.

Gevona glanced at me quickly and then refocused on the road. I didn't think she was going to answer me at all and, when she spoke a good 30 seconds later, she caught me off guard.

"No, I won't be seeing her tonight...or ever."

Now I half turned to face her. "What happened? I mean, if you don't mind me asking? You two seemed like quite an item."

"New Year's Eve, that's what happened."

"Huh?"

"She didn't like that I had to work tonight. Actually, she seemed to think that I could just ask to be moved to day shift, period, and it would happen."

"Yeah, right." I snorted at that.

"Couldn't get her to understand that police work doesn't work that way. And, she didn't like it when I told her the low man on the totem pole definitely gets the short end around major holidays and that on drinking holidays, everybody draws duty."

"So, you broke up over that?"

She shot me a look. "We weren't going steady Janet. We were just dating."

"You know what I mean." I tried to hide my happiness at the whole turn of events.

She didn't pick up on my glee. "Honestly, you couldn't pay me to be out after midnight tonight anyway unless I was working. My mama always called New Year's Eve amateur night. Too many drunk fools on the roads between one and three o'clock."

"Amen!"

We pulled into a package store a couple of blocks away from our Warren Park apartment. It was the only place in the mostly residential area we lived in on the outskirts of downtown Indy that was still open.

After the conversation we'd just had I was surprised at this turn of events and I'm sure it showed in my voice when I asked, "Why are we stopping here?"

"I may not be going out anywhere with anyone tonight but I intend to have a good time.

We don't have to work until tomorrow afternoon; join me?"

"I don't know..."

"We still have about 20, 25 minutes until the ball drops. We can get a bottle of Spumante – I like it better than champagne – and watch that while we wait for a pizza to bake or something."

Taking my agreement for granted, she started to get out of the car. Like a lovesick puppy, I followed.

We counted down with the television announcer and the New York crowd like a couple of school girls then swigged from the glasses we'd hurriedly poured after we got through the door and rushed around getting the broadcast on and a frozen pizza doctored and into the oven. I smiled at Gevona and, to my delight, she smiled back and pulled me in for a quick hug.

"Happy New Year Janet."

"Happy New Year," I said right back to her. She let me go all too soon. Feeling self-conscious now, I took my sparkling wine and retreated a little to the other end of the sofa. She grabbed the TV controller and clicked over to the channel guide, oblivious to my discomfort.

"It just gets stupid from here. Let's see what movies are on."

Scrolling up and down and not finding much of anything playing but New Year's Eve specials, she finally stopped on a channel that was showing 'Dirty Dancing'. "Ooo, it's just starting. Let's watch this!"

"Really?" I was shocked. "I didn't peg you for a Swayze fan."

"Oh girl, that man can dance but it's not about him for me. I like me some Jennifer Gray. I could so do her right now."

I nearly choked on my drink at that.

"You okay?" she asked as she moved quickly to me and started thumping me on the back.

I coughed and sputtered for a couple of seconds but finally managed to choke out, "Stop, stop. I'm fine."

"We can watch something else."

"No, it's fine. I like this movie...I'm...you surprised me, is all. I didn't peg Gray for your type."

"Girl, I don't have a type! I just like women. You oughta know that by now!"

For the next two hours, I quietly got drunk. First on the wine and then, when we'd polished that off, on some coolers we'd had in the fridge for a while. By the time the last dance in the movie came on, I was feeling little pain.

Apparently, Gevona wasn't either. She got up and started bopping and grooving out of time with the mambo scene on the screen. Looking back over her shoulder at me watching her, she laughed and commanded, "Get your drunk ass up and come dance with me."

"You know I don't dance."

"Ain't nobody gonna see you."

"Your logic is flawed your own drunk self. You're here."

"Shut up and come dance."

Getting up reluctantly and with some effort, I wobbled toward her on unsteady feet. I was feeling a little shy and nervous but she started moving towards me too. We just sort of ran into one another and stopped, unsure of what to do next.

I felt my breasts press into Gevona's larger ones and I could feel the heat of her skin through my shirt. Her face was so close to mine; I could smell the wine on her.

Gevona's slid a hand up my back and rested it gently against the back of my neck. Her right hand dropped down and I felt the warmth of her palm pressing against the small of my back. She squeezed gently and I jumped a little, making her laugh.

"What's a matter there Mason; afraid of me?"

Rising to the implied challenge, I wrapped both of my own hands around Gevona's neck. Now our faces were even closer together but, until now, I hadn't been looking directly at her. I didn't really register how close she was until I felt her head tilt slightly to the side and her lips came into contact with my own.

My senses reeled. I pulled back and looked at her but she just smiled at me and moved us into a slow dance that didn't really fit the tempo on the screen.

Her kiss...Even now, it's almost impossible for me to describe what it felt like. I hadn't kissed very many people in my life. Once I figured out my true sexuality in junior high school, I avoided boys like the plague and finding the courage to go looking for a like-minded young female in Zanesville, Ohio completely escaped me. My experiences with women in the Army hardly gave me any real frame of reference.

I had to taste her again. I had to. This time, I went after her. When my lips met hers, I thought I was in heaven but all of that was before I felt Gevona's lips slip open slightly and I felt her breath against my mouth. Instinctively, my own lips parted slightly. I could feel her tongue skitter across my lips. It felt so soft, warm, and sexy that all I could do was open my mouth a little wider to moan.

She slipped her tongue in deeper. My mouth gave way further, inviting her in. I pushed back at her with my own tongue, feeling them roll together. I heard her moan now too and her tongue began to move more quickly inside of my mouth.

I could feel the power of Gevona's kiss all over my body. And I guess it was not just her kiss. I breathed in deeply from my nose and I could smell her scent, her bath gel with a hint of animal lust directly underneath. I could feel her hand on the back of my neck, squeezing with just the right amount of pressure, her soft skin feeling silky against my own. Her other hand moved from my back and gripped my ass tightly, her small fingers sinking in my toned flesh.

I felt my body tightening against Gevona's, making every gap between our bodies shrink as my arms wrapped more tightly around her neck and her arms pulled me tighter. I felt my breasts ache and my body tremble as I felt the friction of Gevona's hardening nipples against my own.

Our heads rocked side to side, both of us trying to gain a better angle so that we could feel more of the incredible sensation. I could have stayed that way forever. But, as suddenly as we had started, it ended.

I suddenly felt Gevona's tongue slip from my mouth, pulling between my teeth and lips. I felt her face pull away from mine and my eyes, then closed, fluttered open. I could see Gevona's beautiful face, her eyes peering at me intently. I felt her begin to pull back slightly. For a moment, I tried to hold her close to me, to feel her heart beat against my chest for a moment longer.

But then, as her body began to move away from mine and the taste of tongue began to cool in my mouth, it felt a little bit like a spell had been broken. Not entirely, of course, I was still feeling the after-effects of her overwhelming sexual energy. My knees felt weak and I was nearly panting, like I had not breathed in a long while. My nipples were straining against my t-shirt and I could tell there was slickness between my legs that was impossible to fake. I looked at her a bit in wonder as she pulled away from me. But the sensation was already fading.

I dropped my hands, which were still sort of up in the air awkwardly, down to my sides. For a moment, I shook my head a bit, trying to get some sort of control over myself. The sensation of Gevona's kiss faded deeper into the past.

Backing away from her, I told her, "I'm so sorry. I...I don't know what came over me."

"I do."

"You do?"

"Baby, I started it, remember?"

"Uh, yeah; but, um, why?"

"Because I wanted to and I think you wanted me to, too."

I didn't say anything. I couldn't speak anymore. In my drunken, sex starved state, I couldn't even think.

Chapter 15

Gevona looked at me and bit her lower lip. "You're horny, aren't you?"

My head dropped and I looked away. She knew at least that much.

"Janet?" she said softly.

When I looked up, she reached out her index finger and hooked it towards her in the universal 'get over here' symbol.

I tried to master my emotions but my body had other ideas. I moved back across the room towards Gevona. She kept her eyes on me as I moved closer to her. I could see the glistening skin on her lips now and I felt my heart ratchet up a few beats per minute. I knew that if I kissed her again, I might slip back into whatever trance I had been in, so I resolved not to do that. I admitted to myself then that there were definitely feelings on my part that might not be returned but I couldn't completely stop myself. All willpower was gone.

Gevona closed her eyes and it was clear she believed I was going in for another kiss. I desperately wanted to do something, anything else. I let my eyes wander over her body, taking in her curves and the smooth softness of her skin. After a brief moment I smiled to myself and realized I knew exactly what I wanted to do.

I took another half step forward and started to bend forward. I dropped my head farther, tilting it towards the side. I had noticed, in allowing my eyes to flit over her taut breasts, that her shirt was incredibly short and tight. I could still see her nipples poking through the sheer fabric and it was clear that she wasn't wearing a bra. When she'd changed out of uniform at work, she must have slipped out of it.

Leaning forward slightly, I opened my mouth, and raised my head. My left hand quickly found its way around Gevona's back, my fingers tickling at her bare spine below the bottom hem of her shirt. At the same instant, my open mouth pressed firmly against the delicious curve on the underside of Gevona's right breast. My tongue moved around the bare flesh and I could feel the velvety sensation of her skin and taste her salty-sweet flavor. At that same instant, my right hand had raised up and come down gently onto Gevona's left breast. My hand wrapped around the fabric of her thin shirt but I could feel the satisfying, surprising weight of her natural breasts against my fingers and I could feel her hardened nipple pressing into my palm.

She let out a surprised groan and I looked up as she looked down at me. I smiled and kept going. I began to suck in gently, pulling more and more of her breast into my mouth. Her skin felt hot and I could feel the blood pumping rapidly beneath it. She felt so smooth under my tongue. I began to move my lips around on the underside of her breast, trying to taste more and more of her salty skin. Meanwhile, my right hand stayed close on Gevona's breast and I began to knead it just slightly, letting my fingers dance across her. I could feel her body squirming slightly and she let out a soft moan.

She reached behind her back and lifted the little shirt over her head. I kept moving my lips, sliding them up from the underside of her breast. After a moment, I felt the slight change in texture as my lips passed over the edge of her areola. I could feel the hard nub of her nipple as it began to press against my top lip. I kept sucking and pulling, feeling the tension rise in her skin.

I groaned as I came to terms with the fact that I was sucking on Gevona's nipple. I couldn't believe how it felt. It tasted sweeter than the rest of her breasts and the firm texture was amazing to me. I sucked harder, pulling more of her nipple into my mouth. Now it was resting on my tongue, the skin stretching taut. I flicked my tongue against it, feeling it bounce and vibrate. She moaned and her back arched.

We stayed in that position in the living room for quite a long time. I just kept sucking and flicking at her nipple and kneading and massaging her breast. She moaned and her body shook against me. My mind and my body was focused on the smell of her body, the feel of her breast, the taste of her nipple, and the sound of her moans, but an unconscious part of me was focused somewhere else.

That part of me controlled my left hand, which was still wrapped around her back. It snaked down and around, almost on its own, and found the waistline of her jeans. I worked the button and zipper and then tugged them down gently.

Slowly I moved my hand and my lips from Gevona's breasts. I stood up straight now and took a step or so backwards.

She was still standing with her hands at her sides, her back arched slightly. Her breasts were pointing out proudly and her stomach looked flat and toned. But my eyes were now drawn down. Just as she hadn't been wearing a bra, she hadn't been wearing any panties under her jeans.

Her legs were spread apart slightly and, at my close distance, I could see it all. She was shaved completely bare. I could see her hard clit sitting up high on the top and I could see all of her skin glistening with excitement.

Now that there was some distance between us, physically at least, I tried to gain my bearings. I spent a little more time trying to talk myself into believing that I was not really feeling the things I was feeling as I looked at Gevona's nude body. I told myself that nothing had been scrambled in my brain by her kiss. I even tried to tell myself that we were simply having a little fun and that it was nothing more than that.

My own wanton need compelled me to keep going. Gevona evidentially felt the same way and, once again, she made the first move. She took a step towards me and the distance between us shrank. Our chests were only a few inches apart and she was looking directly into my eyes.

For a brief moment, she paused. Then, in an incredibly quick and dexterous movement, she sort of pounced on me and stripped my own t-shirt off of me quickly. My sports bra followed in short order. My nipples hardened on their own. They didn't seem to need any more help from her aside from her hasty undressing of them.

She wasn't finished. Taking complete control over me in my love sick, sex starved, wine induced haze, she draped her right arm loosely over my shoulder while her left arm snaked between my arm and the side of my body. I felt her forearm just barely brush against the side of my breast as both of her hands emerged on the backside of my body. Her arms locked together loosely, holding me in a tight hug. I prepared for another staggering kiss, but she had another idea. She found my neck and pressed her warm mouth against it, kissing it gently.

I moaned slightly at that sensation.

I felt our bodies press together once again. I could feel the soft skin of her belly against mine as she rubbed herself against my denim covered thigh. I could certainly feel the heat rushing between my legs.

I started working on removing my own jeans and panties. When she caught on to what I was doing, her lips stayed on my neck but her hands joined mine to help me finish the job.

When they were off, she went right back to sucking gently on my neck but, with her weight mostly on me now, she took a step between my legs with her right leg. The action caused her to crouch slightly and I felt her nipples slip down my breasts. I also felt her weight start to pull me down. With her leg wrapped around my own, I couldn't take a step back to catch my balance. My moan turned into a surprised sharp intake of breath instead as I began to trip backwards, instead.

I felt Gevona's right hand slip up my shoulder and gently cradle my neck. Her left hand wrapped around my waist and she held me close. I still fell backwards, but I could feel her strong arms holding me up. I bent my knees slightly as I started to fall, allowing her to catch me. I arched my back slightly and then sat gently on my butt. I could feel her leg unlace from mine. In a few moments we both ended up on the floor. I was lying on my back, the weight of Gevona's body on top of me. I could still feel her pussy kissing my leg, now silky with the removal of my jeans.

We lay together in that way for a few moments while my body reacted powerfully to her embrace. I felt my nipples growing harder as the pressure of Gevona's warm, soft body on top of me increased. I could feel my own pussy now, though the fabric of my panties, pressing deliciously against her thigh.

I'm not sure how long I simply allowed her to keep kissing my neck. When she started doing something different, it was so subtle that I didn't even notice right away. I was simply enjoying the sensation of being touched. I didn't even bother to try and tell myself anymore that we were just having a little fun at that point. I wasn't even really thinking about the larger implications or anything else that really mattered to me in that moment.

I felt her soft, supple lips kiss my clavicle, the top of my breast, and my breastbone as she slowly began to move her lips down my body. As she pulled herself back, her breasts continued to slide down my own, increasing the friction on my aching nipples. Eventually, her breasts slipped off of mine and I could feel them against my belly. At the same time, I could feel her pussy slipping down my thigh. I gasped as her thigh moved out from between my legs and the beautiful friction on me dissipated but soon my attention returned to her lips. She was moving slightly faster now and I could feel her face moving down, down, between my breasts. I could feel her smooth cheeks as they actually brushed the sides of my breasts and against my hardened nipple. I moaned and rolled my head on the floor.

Her mouth opened wider and her tongue splayed out wet and thick on my breast. She moved her head that last inch over and I felt her rough, soft tongue splay across my desperate nipple. I sucked in air quickly and I felt all of my muscles tighten. I couldn't believe how much sensation her lick shot through my body. My toes tingled and the hair on the back of my neck stood on end.

Her tongue swirled around my nipple a few more times and then her mouth closed around it. I gasped as I felt her begin to suck gently on my nipple, pulling it deep into her mouth and flicking it with her tongue.

So caught up was I, I didn't realize that her fingers hand slipped lower until I felt her stroke through my hair. My legs spread a little farther apart and I felt a desperate need for someone or something to touch my exposed center.

She kissed my nipple once more, making me shudder. Then she once again began to trail her lips down my body. She left an unbroken chain of kisses down along the underside of my breast, across my stomach to my bellybutton and then down, slowly, between my legs.

I'm not sure how long it took for her to make this journey, but it felt like hours. Every place her lips touched felt like fire after she left, but the sensations against my skin were no longer what held my attention. I was leaning forward slightly, looking down between my breasts. My eyes were wide and I was staring intently at the top of her head. I could see the gentle curves of her body, the swell of her ass, her lithe legs. I could not think of anything else except for staying focused on her body. I knew what was about to happen and the anticipation was nearly overwhelming. If her mere kiss had taken my breath away, what would happen now?

I felt her lips press against the skin a few inches directly below my bellybutton just above my aching clit. Her head moved side to side briefly and I saw a shoulder drop slightly.

Without further warning I felt it. Her pouty, wet lips had come into contact with my core. My muscles tightened further and I heard myself groan. She had placed the gentlest pressure on the dripping center of my slit, her nose just fractions of an inch from my clit. Her lips sunk into me softly and I could feel them caressing my over-stimulated skin. She kept the kiss there for a moment and then briefly moved her lips away from me. I sighed in disappointment. But before I could even absorb my desperate need for more, I felt her lips once again press into my lips, a little farther down this time.

She continued in this manner patiently, slowly dropping kisses down the length of my pussy, never pressing hard. Her lips were now soaked with my arousal and they lubricated her kisses, making them feel even more silky.

I was soon overwhelmed by the scent of our arousal. It seemed to fill the entire room as it wrapped us together in a sensual embrace.

Occasionally, her tongue would dart out of her mouth, giving just the slightly penetration to her kiss. Despite the increased intensity, she didn't move any faster. She eked her way up and down my pussy, causing my body to shake and my breath to stop multiple times. When she reached the mid-point of my aching slit on a trail back up, instead of working downward again as she had been, she kept moving up, bringing her lips closer and closer to my desperate clit.

With the top of her lip just barely avoiding contact with my clit, she suddenly stopped. She kept her lips planted against my slit. I saw her eyes flash open and they actually looked up at me from between my legs. Her eyes glittered and I could not tell if they looked aroused or feverish; maybe both. We locked eyes for a long time, my body trembling and my muscles taut under her body.

Finally, she seemed satisfied that I was absolutely desperate. She moved her lips back away from my body and started to move her head forward again as though she was going to plant another delicate kiss, only this time on my clit. But just before her lips touched me, they split open. Her warm, writhing tongue dropped heavily out of her mouth and splashed with full force against it. Her tongue wrapped over my clit instantly in a thick, soft mass and drenched it.

I gasped, my body was overwhelmed by the sudden sensation. All I knew was that the tension had suddenly ratcheted up a couple of hundred percent and I knew that I needed something to release the pressure. Then I felt her palm glide across my breast and I felt her fingers wrap around me, digging into my throbbing flesh. In moments, she was kneading the relieved flesh of my breast with her fingers and gently teasing my tight nipple with her palm.

There was no time to savor this feeling because, at nearly the same moment, the full effect of her tongue working on my clit came into focus. Her tongue swirled around on me loosely and made my toes curl. I sighed deeply as all my nerve endings tingled and my bones turned to jelly.

We stayed there in that position on the floor for quite some time. I honestly don't know how long. I just remember that she kept kneading my breast and licking at my clit with concentrated attention. I don't know how she did it, but she managed to push me further and further into delirium, my juices dripping onto her chin, but she always managed to back off before I could cum. The sensation was simultaneously invigorating and maddening. My body flailed on the floor and I could hear my voice moaning but, I was so far gone, it didn't even really sound like me.

I gasped when she suddenly changed positions. Without stopping her tongue for more than a second or two, she let go of my breast and flipped her body position around on the floor and then mounted me backwards.

Taking my cue, I reached up and took hold of her hips gently, then pulled her center toward me. She arched slightly and repositioned her knees. I giggled low at the feeling of her clitoris rubbing against my nose and breathed in deeply; then I moaned as the full effect of her scent overwhelmed my senses. I could feel my own clit aching between my legs.

Opening my mouth, I instantly felt her silky pussy lips rub against my tongue. I heard Gevona moaning as I started to slide my tongue up and down her dripping slit.

Her taste was unbelievable. Her juices were very thick and salty and sweet, all at the same time. I made my tongue rigid and, just like she was doing to me; I pushed my tongue inside of her. She screamed out and her hips rocked, driving her pussy down hard on my face and pushing my tongue further into her body.

After several minutes of licking her delicious slit, I tilted my head back slightly and soon my lips were wrapped around her hard clit. Her muscles went tense as I kissed her sensitive little bead of nerves, letting my tongue skitter out of my mouth and lick at it. After a moment, I sucked in slightly, pulling Gevona's clit between my lips and into my mouth. I started to flick it gently with my tongue, rubbing my taste buds all around her smooth, dense flesh. Her entire body reacted to every movement of my tongue.

While she was distracted with the feeling of it all, I carefully raised my right hand up towards my chin. Her pussy was so incredibly wet at this point from my saliva and from her own arousal that I didn't even need to stick my fingers inside of her to get them wet. Instead, I moved my index finger and my middle finger around in the wet opening of her slit, coating it in her juices.

My tongue was still wildly swirling on her clit as I pulled my dripping fingers back away from her pussy.

"Oh no you don't, fuck me!" Gevona yelled as her body began to shake wildly.

We were both way, way too far gone to maintain any level of control over our actions. I obliged her request and she thrust her hips hard against me, grinding in a forceful and unmerciful manner.

All of the muscles in my own body tightened up and my breath caught in my throat. I could feel her muscles tensing against me too. I knew that she was feeling what I was feeling. That realization sent me careening over the edge.

The only thing in the world was the sensation tearing through my body as I pleasured her and she returned the favor. For several long seconds, I was in a daze. As my foggy haze finally began to lift slightly, I could feel Gevona's body quaking. My own body did the same. My orgasm was powerful and hers seemed to be too. I felt like we were sharing a real connection and that it felt like something that could be so much more than just sex.

Chapter 16

10:37 AM, Sunday, January 1st, 2012

I'm not used to drinking more than a glass or two of wine in an evening. Since I'd downed several, my morning 'wine headache' was severe. The sunlight streaming into the room from the blinds I'd never flipped closed in my sex crazed state the night before also did nothing to help my pain.

I was lying on my right side, facing toward the window, much as I always did. I started to roll to my back but I was stopped by a firm, warm wall behind me. Realization dawned; Gevona was still in my bed.

Sometime well into the night, we'd shifted from the living room to my bedroom and continued our lovemaking. Even in my alcohol induced, morning pain, I smiled to myself at the memory.

Shifting a little, I quickly came to realize, headache or not, I needed to pee but I didn't want to disturb her. She was snoring very softly. In the years that we'd lived together and shared space, I'd never heard her do it before. Of course, I thought, I'd never shared a bed with her before or even ventured into her room when she was sleeping.

All of that is about to change, I thought to myself. We made a real connection last night, the two of us.

Instead of getting up, taking care of my urgent need, and trying to find some ibuprofen, I decided to play the loving girlfriend. I rolled onto my left side and spooned my new lover from behind.

My actions instantly woke Gevona up. *So much for trying not to disturb her.*

From her position lying on her own left side, she started to push herself up but she paused before trying to swing her legs sideways off of the bed. Her head swiveled as if she was taking in my room for the first time and then she looked back at me. To my eyes, her face showed a mixture of hangover pain and curiosity.

Conscious of how bad my breath probably was, I gave her a slight smile and said softly, "Good morning beautiful."

The effect of my greeting was startling, to say the least. She turned away, rose from the bed and, pulling the sheet out from under the blanket and around her as she went, she retreated into my bathroom.

I sat up and scratched my head, puzzled by her reaction. I wasn't sure if she was upset or if she just needed to use the facilities before she could form a rational thought. My own need to do the same came rushing back to me.

Since she was in my bathroom, I skipped across the hall to hers and used it quickly.

Unsure about what to do next, I thought a little modesty was probably the best policy so I grabbed panties, sweatpants and a t-shirt and quickly put them on.

There wasn't a sound coming from the bathroom. "Gevona," I called out, "is everything okay?"

Her answer, "Be out in a few minutes," was several beats in coming.

I paced my own floor for several seconds, debating whether I should wait right there for her or give her some space. My headache solved the problem for me. I left her to herself and went to the kitchen in search of medication and coffee.

Once the coffee was brewing, I spun away from the back counter and faced back toward the hallway in time to see my roommate turned lover dart from my room, naked, across the hall to her room. When I didn't hear her door close though, I breathed out the breath I didn't even realize I'd been holding. Modesty, I thought, seems to be the rule of the morning but I didn't feel any sort of a vibe that told me Gevona was upset.

My confidence boosted, I called out to her, "Coffee will be ready in just a minute," then I busied myself getting out the mugs, the cream and sweetener that she liked and the real sugar that I liked.

She appeared, dressed much the same way I was, as I was taking my first tentative sip of the hot brew. I held up her cup to her and she moved toward me and took it, smiling gratefully.

We sipped away in what I thought was just ratcheted up a notch from our usual companionable silence. Breaking the spell, I asked, "So how are you feeling? Do you need ibuprofen because, if you do, there's some in the cupboard." I jerked my thumb back over my shoulder toward the kitchen cupboard we used as a sort of community medicine chest for basics like Tylenol, bandages and antacid.

She shook her head no. "I'm fine, just a little tired."

I snickered at that; couldn't help myself.

She shot me a look then that could have melted glass.

Uh oh, time to do a little damage control.

"Sorry. I didn't mean that to sound...wasn't laughing at you but at..."

Gevona held a hand up to me. "We're both adults here and we're both cops, right?"

I nodded.

"Just spit it out then. What's on your mind?"

Her words weren't said with venom but I detected an edge to her voice that wasn't usually there, even on the job, in tense situations. I opted for honesty as the best policy.

"I love you," I told her simply.

Her response was quick and lighthearted, "Girl, I love you too." She offered up the buddy fist bump with the hand that wasn't holding a coffee mug.

She didn't get it. I tried again. "I'm in love with you Gevona; have been for months." The words just kept tumbling out, all in a rush. "Last night was amazing. I feel like we really connected. I just know you felt it too. Now, I know we've lived together a long time..."

"Stop, stop," she tried to interrupt me.

I couldn't stop; I needed to get everything I was thinking out. "We've been roommates but not lovers. All our friends and co-workers see us as just that – friends and coworkers. We don't have to change that, not for now anyway. Not until we get comfortable with this change in our relationship and we're both ready to reveal it."

Gevona turned away from me and set her cup down on the breakfast island. She braced both hands against it and stared into the kitchen for several long seconds while I stood by, leaning against the dining table we had off to one side of the main room so that it sort of divided the kitchen from the living room, and waited for her response, any response.

When she finally spoke, her voice had lost its usual assuredness; it tremored and cracked a little. The first words that came from her throat were certainly not what I wanted to hear.

She said, "Janet, I don't want to hurt you. I love you very much. Love like a best friend. Love like a sister in arms...in more ways than one. We go back, girl. But, I'm not in love with you baby. I'm just not."

Sighing, she continued when I didn't respond, "I've felt a different sort of vibe from you for the last couple of months and now I know why. I'm just sorry I didn't see it sooner."

What she was saying finally registered. "But, but," now my own voice trembled, "last night?"

She blew out a heavy breath and shook her head at me. "Last night was a mistake. A mistake on my part. You were drunk and I was horny and I lost control...but, there's no excuse. I took advantage of you and I shouldn't have and I deeply, deeply regret what I did."

"Deeply, deeply, huh?" I was mad now. "So, you're trying to tell me that it was just sex and all in fun; that it meant absolutely nothing to you?"

"No, that's not what I meant. Look, we're friends. I don't want to lose that with you but..."

I cut her off. "I get it Gevona, friends 'with benefits'. I totally see what your angle is."

"You're twisting my words! That's not what I meant at all. Arrrgh!" she yelled in frustration.

My anger continued unabated. "I thought you were different!" I yelled at her. "Now I'm seeing that you're just like Kyra and...and..." I was at a loss. In my limited experience, I really didn't really have anyone else to compare her to.

"No. You're wrong. Kyra used *everybody*. She never committed to a soul. I should know, Janet...she used me too."

That revelation took my anger down a notch. I moved from my position still near the table to the couch and sank down on it. Leaning forward, I put my head in my hands and rubbed my scalp hard with my fingers.

Gevona must have moved from the island into the living room area. Her voice came from somewhere out in front of me, her tone softer now, almost soothing. "I'm sorry. I really am and I hope that we can get past this and still be friends. You're my rock Janet Mason; the one steady thing in my life."

Chapter 17

March 12ᵗʰ, 2012
Warren Park, Indiana

"We need to talk."

"About?" I asked her as I peeled off my jacket and hung it on the back of the door and then waited while Gevona did the same.

"About me...about us."

"There is no 'us'," I remarked back to her, while trying to keep my tone even. Turning away from her at that, I walked out of the little entry hall and headed toward the kitchen. It was late, but our habit had always been to eat something after shift. Lots of things had changed in the last couple of months but that hadn't.

"I knew you would make this hard."

"Make what hard? I've done nothing the last couple of months but try to get over myself and stay friends with you. You've been aloof and downright standoffish." I said my piece matter-of-factly because I really believed it was true. She'd been distant ever since our falling out on New Year's Day. We still shared rides to and from work but they were often made in stilted silence.

Thank heaven we don't patrol in pairs! I couldn't stand to be partnered up with her right now!

Figuring on just throwing things for a sandwich together, I was peering into the fridge when she came into the kitchen behind me.

"Are you listening to me?"

"Yes," I answered but I kept digging.

"I wanted you to be the first to know...after the Sheriff that is; I took a patrol job with Indy. I handed in my resignation tonight."

I bumped my head on the upper part of the fridge where it meets the freezer as I pulled out of the box quickly. "You what?" I asked her as I rubbed the back of my head hard to try and dissipate the pain.

"I gave him two weeks' notice."

"How long have you been working on that?"

"Not as long as you think."

"I'm not thinking anything right now Gevona; I'm just trying to process it."

"Indy isn't technically hiring right now. They do interviews on a rolling basis, as needed though for experienced cops. Lacy Baumgarten got on there and she recommended me. Remember her from when we first started patrol?"

When I just shrugged, she went on. "I got an interview and I got on."

"That's what you want?"

She nodded. "I've always wanted to be on a big department, work my way up. We talked about that a long time ago. This," she waved her hand around, "Hancock, was my foot in the door."

"I see." That's what I said to her, but I really didn't see. We were busy in Hancock County and Gevona was a good Deputy. *This has something to do me; she's not fooling anybody but herself.*

"We're both getting ready to sit for the Detective exam. You do well, you have a real shot to move up with Hancock now. You know you're going to start right back at the bottom again in Indy."

She looked away from me and mumbled something.

"What? I didn't catch that."

"I said, that's not all."

"What's not all?" I was confused and my head still hurt making me just want to sit down. I moved around the island and perched on one of the stools.

Gevona stayed in the kitchen but turned to face me from across the countertop. I watched as she took a deep breath and blew it out. "I'm just going to say it; I'm moving out."

I couldn't speak. I just stared at her.

"Janet? Janet? Say something."

I have no idea how long we sat like that as I tried to process her latest salvo. Realizing I was about to cry and not wanting her to see me, I got up, turned away from her and, tossing "Good luck" over my shoulder, I retreated to my room to be alone in my misery.

###

March 30th, 2012
Steak & Shake

"Girl, you've got to snap out of it, she's gone and she ain't comin' back."

I dipped a shoestring fry in ketchup and popped it in my mouth. It was already cold. They're so thin, they don't stay hot long if you let them sit. I pushed the side plate of them away and focused back on my steak-burger.

Reggie tried again, "We need to get you out to the club or something; get you back among the living."

I looked at him shook my head no. "No clubs. You know that's not my scene."

"Honey, you met me in a club."

"Wrong; Gevona met you in a club. We," I pointed at him and then back at myself, "just hit it off better."

I thought back to that night nearly a year ago when she'd been dancing with him at a club while I was trying to coral a wannabe rapist. The drag queen and she had exchanged numbers with platitudes to each other to 'hang out sometime' and we'd all three ended up getting together. But, as Reggie rather than Regina, Gevona didn't have a lot of interest in him and soon it was just the two of us getting together.

"Girlfriend, you know I love you. You know I want what's best for you, right?"

"Yes."

"She wasn't the one for you. She liked women that were crazy in and out of the sack, not level headed steady ones like you."

"You say that like it's a bad thing."

"It's not. My point is, on the job she was in control and level headed, am I right?"

He didn't wait for me to respond. "She didn't want the same thing at home baby doll. You two were always better as friends and co-workers and whatnot than you ever would have been as a couple."

I didn't see it that way.

Chapter 18

November, 2013
Hancock County, Indiana

I thought patrol was busy. It had nothing on being a Detective in training. I could only imagine my workload when the Sheriff turned me loose to work cases on my own.

I threw myself into my work because I knew I was lucky to be there at all. After Gevona left, I didn't even want to sit for the department's detective exam. I couldn't see the point.

Reggie was the one who convinced me, finally, that if I couldn't let go of my thoughts of her, I at least needed to think about my future too. He seemed to be the only friend that I still had. Some of those that stopped calling and texting and dropping by called me a workaholic because I started picking up all of the shifts I could leaving me with less and less time to spend with them and still others said I was obsessed with someone I couldn't have. I didn't care.

What surprised me most were the women on and off the department we used to hang out with that drifted away from me but remained friends with her as if it was me that somehow had wronged her. They talked about me behind my back and shunned me to my face. I pretended I didn't care but it hurt losing them and having them act like that as much as it had hurt having

Gevona just walk out of my life...as much as losing her.

Stopping myself, I reminded myself for what was probably the hundredth time; you never really had her.

###

5:45 PM, March, 18th, 2014
Hancock County, IN

The body was still warm; the gunshot wound to his chest fresh with blood that hadn't yet started to congeal. The victim hadn't been dead long.

There was nothing but corn and soy fields on both sides of I-40 in the area I was in, for the moment, between Greenfield and Indy. If patrol hadn't stopped to investigate the older model Lincoln parked slightly cockeyed on the berm, the man probably wouldn't have been found until morning. Darkness was coming fast.

I got up from my crouch as the coroner approached and gave him and his team room to do their jobs. The car was my primary piece of evidence now and I was wasting daylight.

Had to be drugs, I thought to myself as I popped open the trunk from the dash and then walked around to the back to have a look. It was empty save for a nearly bald spare tire, a crappy little jack and a tire iron. It wasn't clean though.

The carpeting inside was covered in grass clippings, dirt, lint and who knows what all else.

"Forensics will have their work cut out for them with this," I said out loud into the dusk.

My attention was drawn to a vehicle pulling off the road behind me. Self-preservation instincts kicking in, even though there were two patrol units still on the scene with me along with the Coroner, I moved around to the side of the vehicle and out of the line of impact.

Relief flooded through me when Warren McDonnell got out of the unfamiliar vehicle. I hadn't been able to tell it was the Sheriff coming onto the scene in the waning evening light.

He grinned as he walked toward me. "Had ya' wondering didn't I?" he asked as he waved his arm at the sedan he'd stepped out of. My wife's new car. It was the first one out. What do we have?"

"Judging by the scene, the murder victim was targeted. There's enough left front end damage to indicate he was run off the road by something even bigger than this thing. I'm thinking he was running drugs and somebody that was aware of that ran him down, robbed him of his cargo and killed him to keep him quiet."

"It's an odd vehicle for that."

"How so, Sheriff?"

"A Lincoln Town Car? Maybe back in the '70s or '80s but, these days, they're so unusual they stand out, especially these older models that are big as tanks. It would draw too much attention from patrol just about anywhere. Any dealer or mule worth his salt would know that."

"Guess I hadn't thought of it like that." I berated myself silently.

"You could be right Mason but my hunch is something else was going on with this one. We'll just have to investigate all the angles now, won't we?"

"Yes sir." *I learn something new every day.*

He moved forward to get a look at the front of the car. My personal cell buzzed in my pocket. I didn't dare pull it out with him here.

2:10 PM, March 21st, 2014
Warren Park, Indiana

"I've been trying to reach you for a few days now."

"I know Aunt Leslie. Work is crazy right now what with me training as a detective and...and, just being as crazy busy as it always is. I'm so sorry."

She skipped right over my apology. "You can drop the 'Aunt' hon. We're all adults now."

I didn't really feel comfortable calling her Leslie, even though she was my favorite aunt. My mother had always pushed me to be so polite and formal with everyone in the family that just the thought of only calling her 'Leslie' was odd to me.

"Janet, your mama wouldn't call you; that's why I am."

"Is something wrong?"

"That's just it; she's been feeling poorly for a while. I finally convinced her to see her family doctor a couple of weeks ago."

That old quack, I thought to myself.

"He referred her out to a cancer doctor in Columbus. We took her over there to the James where they ran a bunch of tests on her."

"And?" I swallowed hard. My mom and I still didn't see eye to eye about a lot of things but I love her and, deep down, I know she really loves me. I wasn't at all prepared to hear about a medical diagnosis of cancer or anything else, on any level. I sank into the chair adjacent to the couch and clutched my phone tightly as Aunt Leslie poured out the details of what little they knew so far.

When she paused for a breath, I interjected, "How long?"

Sighing, she told me, "They don't know for sure dear. They're going to start her on Chemo but she's far enough advanced that it's probably too late to do a whole lot more than slow the progression. She might have six months; she might have a couple of years. They won't speculate beyond that."

Chapter 19

Sunday Evening, October 19th, 2014

I hate I-70! Such a boring drive!
I'd stopped picking up extra shifts and working extended overtime. I'd been spending every 36-48 hour break I could get for months commuting between Indy and Zanesville after coming to terms with the fact that it was time to make amends and be with my mother as much as possible while she was still on this earth.

As I stared straight ahead into a long stretch of nothing, I thought about this latest visit home. Saturday, mom was doing okay. We'd gotten out and about a little bit to enjoy a beautiful fall day. This morning, I'd had to call Aunt Leslie away from church services to come and help me as mom had started to have a really bad spell.

It tore my heart out to leave with her in that state but I had an early morning shift and cases backlogged for miles. I had to get home and try to get some rest so I could go at the job fresh, with a clear head.

The job...love it, but I'm beat. "I can't keep doing this," I said out loud. The announcer on the radio didn't respond to me; he just continued with his pitch.

Friday, November 28th, 2014

Muskingum County Sheriff's Department
Zanesville, Ohio

"Zanesville is my hometown. I'd be really happy to get back here finally; if you hire me that is, Sheriff."

The woman sitting behind the desk knitted her brows and peered at me closely. "Why don't you tell me a little about your career, Mason?" she asked me. "Your record here only covers your time with your current department."

"Well, there isn't a whole lot beyond that to tell, is why," I responded, ashamed to hear my voice tremor a little. "I'm actually only 30."

Now Sheriff Crane's eyebrows rose but she schooled her features very quickly. I still caught her look of surprise and I chuckled. My confidence boosted, I launched into the mini version of my story.

"I grew up in Zanesville. Right after high school, I went to Zane State and got an Associates in criminal justice. I was only 20 by the time I finished that though and I couldn't get a job in law enforcement in Ohio...I couldn't even get into OPOTA, sponsored or not."

Crane nodded.

"Basically, I did they only thing I could do at the time to get police work, I joined the Army. I did my four years as a Military Police Officer and got out."

"How'd you end up in Indiana instead of back here?"

"A, uh...buddy I served with was from Indy and convinced me to apply to Hancock County; said they needed more women on the department. My mom and I weren't on the best of terms then anyway. I wasn't ready to move back home, right then, so I took the plunge to be completely on my own." I knew it was a slight distortion of the whole truth but I was trying to keep any thoughts of anything having to do with Gevona completely out of my mind.

"And now?"

I wasn't sure what she was asking but she rephrased her own question, "You're ready to come home now?"

"I'll be honest; my mom is sick...cancer, among other things...she can't work anymore. She's getting where she can't do much of anything but get out of bed some days. Other days...well, she's almost normal. I want to be back here for as many of those 'almost normal' days as I can be."

"This job isn't a nine to five deal; you know?"

"Completely. I didn't expect anything less and I don't expect any special treatment. My mother's older sister Leslie...my aunt Leslie Toth...cares for mom most of the time when she can't do for herself. Her and her husband Bob live right here in town too."

"Alright then," she shifted gears again, "let's talk more about your career with Hancock County."

"Right; I applied there coming out of the Army and got picked up by them right away. They sent me straight to the academy."

Sheriff Crane glanced down at my paperwork and then asked, "You went right out on the road after you graduated then, I take it?"

"Actually no, I did my year as a jailer just like everyone else does...but to the day. As soon as I had three-sixty-five in, they put me on the street. My uh Army buddy wasn't kidding; they needed to bring more women on board because there was a lawsuit against them for unfair hiring practices towards women."

Wincing, Melissa Crane shook her head. "Bet that was fun!"

I shrugged in response, "It was fine. The Sheriff that was there lost in the next election. The new guy turned the whole department around."

"So, that's what, four...five years on the road?"

Nodding, she told me, "I sat for the detective exam early in my fourth year on the road with the department. I passed and got pretty high on the list. I made detective sergeant not quite a year later."

"That's fast!"

"It's a pretty big department, Sheriff with some turnover. I mean, Hancock's population isn't quite as high as Muskingum County's but, being so close to Indy; it's pretty busy, especially with patrol and all the crap we had to deal with just rolling through trying to get to the city. People get a couple years there under their belt there and then they apply to Indy's police department or to State." I started to shake my head at the memory of Gevona doing exactly that but I controlled the urge.

"I know your Sheriff."

"McDonnell?"

Crane nodded. "Yes. Things are rough all along the I-70 corridor. We met at a conference in St. Louis last year for Sheriff's in the region when I was still wet behind the ears as the Sheriff here. It okay if I give him a call?"

I nodded at her. "Yes ma'am. He's well aware of my situation and that I'm looking for a position closer to home."

Part Three
Love at 'First' Sight?

Chapter 20

Janet
Tuesday Evening, December 23rd, 2014
Boar's Head Bar

I walked into the bar and looked around. Mel waving at me from half way across the room caught my attention. As I moved toward the table where she was sitting with several other women, I thought I vaguely recognized a few of the faces dotted around the room. Several people from the department were hanging out, relaxing.

"Have a seat. Janet," Mel offered. "You know Holly and my wife Dana. This is my sister Kris."

As I sat down, I stuck out my hand to Mel's sister and offered, "Nice to meet you Kris." Something struck me just then and I did a double take. "Hey, wait a minute!" escaped unbidden from my mouth.

The other three women laughed.

"You're pretty quick," Kris said. "Not everyone picks up on it right away since we wear our hair different and all."

"She's a detective; she better be quick," Mel told her twin.

"How are you liking it working with Mel, so far?" Kris asked me.

We'd spent some cold evenings on stakeouts and I was still feeling a little under the weather.

My body picked that exact moment to have a coughing spell as I tried to respond. "It's...um...fine," I rasped.

"Are you all right? It doesn't sound like it's been fine." Kris shot Mel a look.

Coming to her own defense, Mel told her, "We got off to a bit of a rocky start but everything's good now."

Still not able to talk, I smiled instead, saying 'thanks' with my eyes.

"Okay, here we go," a woman said, as she stopped at the table and placed a beer in front of Dana and then a daiquiri in front of Kris. "And, you've added another I see."

"Barb, this is Janet," Mel said. "Janet, Barb owns this place now and she's done an amazing job cleaning it up. It used to be a real pit and responsible for a lot of our evening and weekend business."

"I was admiring it when I came in; very nice."

"Well thanks! So you're a deputy too?" Barb asked me.

"Detective. I've only been with the department a couple of weeks...moved back home from Indiana. I grew up here in Zanesville."

"What's your last name?"

"Mason. Yours?"

"I'm back to using Wysocki...what everyone knows me by around here. Where did you go to school Janet Mason?"

"I went to Zanesville and to COTC after that."

"Hmm. Well, I'm sorry I'm being so nosy but you look so familiar to me," Barb said to me.

"You look familiar to me too."

"Ahem," Mel cleared her throat; "I hate to break up this game of 20 questions but I think those guys over there are trying to get your attention Barb." She pointed to a group of guys that had come in just after me and took up residence a couple of tables over.

She looked in the direction Mel was pointing and then turned quickly back to me, "What can I get you to drink hon?"

"Whatever's light on draft."

"Be right back."

Barb moved over to the table of guys and spent a couple of minutes talking with them and taking their orders. She returned shortly and placed my draft down, telling me, "I'm not done quizzing you yet."

She continued over to deliver two pitchers and a round of shots to the table of men and hung there for another minute as they talked with her some more. I watched, curious as she looked our way, laughed and looked back at the guys. Concentrating hard in the din of conversation, jukebox music and pool balls clacking, I heard her laughingly tell them, "I don't think you want to do that...it's a table of mostly married women and all but one of them are cops but, I'll ask them if you want."

A protest rose up from the table and I chuckled as Barb sidled back over to us.

"Ladies," she said, her back to the other table, "you almost had a round of drinks on them but right now they're over there playing a game of 'who's not the cop.'"

"Technically," Dana put in, "two of us aren't."

"Oh honey," Barb replied, "you may not be serving right now but everything about you screams cop."

Mel tipped her head just slightly toward Holly who was between the two of us and said to Barb, "Maybe they should be playing a game of who's the only one who's both straight *and* single."

"Is that right?" Barb asked, her eyes on me rather than on Holly.

"Look who's getting cozy over at the bar," Holly said.

Mel turned that way in time to see Barb walking away from the end where Janet sat, laughing at something that had transpired between them. She smiled.

Dana moved up beside her wife and nudged her, "What's got you grinning over here?" She looked in the direction Mel was looking.

The couple watched as Barb handed a beer across to a customer, took his money and put it in the till and then moved right back to Janet.

"That could work," Mel said. "They both need somebody new in their lives."

"I'll be surprised if it goes beyond a night of casual conversation," Dana replied. "Barb is still grieving badly over Lisa's death."

"And Janet is living her grieving in advance over the loss of what her mother once was and will never be again. They could help each other through their grief."

###

Janet
At the bar

"So, what were you doing before you took this place over?"

"The same thing, more or less. This is what I've been doing...we were doing, for the past dozen years, give or take; buying crappy bars and turning them into places where people *want* to go and hang out." She sort of half smiled like she was remembering something.

I picked up on the word 'we' and I remembered her remark about using the name 'Wysocki' now that she was back in town so, being the nosy detective that I was becoming, I zeroed in on that.

"So, I take it you're divorced now and you came back here to get away from him?"

"Way off the mark, detective." She smiled just a little bigger at me.

"Oh, sorry. I do that – jump to conclusions – sometimes; bad in my line of work, I know. I'm still learning all of the ins and outs of the investigative side of the job."

"You haven't done many interrogations, have you?"

I shook my head no. "Not yet, in all honesty. I'm sure I'll have plenty of those ahead of me in my career."

She laughed at that. "If that isn't the God's truth working with Mel!" At that, a customer got her attention and she moved away to serve him.

I took the time to study her features a little more closely while she was otherwise occupied. When she finished getting his order, no one else needed her attention so she pulled another draught and returned to the end of the bar where she placed it in front of me and picked up the almost empty glass I'd been sipping on since I'd arrived an hour before.

"I'm driving, you know."

"Been in this business a long time Janet Mason. Two beers in two hours with your build isn't going to have you staggering out of here drunk."

Before I could frame a response above and beyond a rueful grin, she told me, "Don't think I didn't know you were watching me a minute ago. I could feel your eyes."

"Another trick of the trade?" I teased her.

"Something like that."

"I just have the gut feeling we've met somewhere before, is all. Where were you before you came back to Ohio...if you don't mind my asking, that is?"

"Colorado, for far longer than I should have been."

"Oh. It didn't go so well?"

She leaned into the bar, toward me a little. "The bar business there was fine. We were in a resort area...can't for the life of me figure out why the previous owner of the place was failing miserably and had to sell."

She trailed off, seemingly lost in thought. I stayed quiet and sipped on the fresh draught.

"I lost my wife out there...complications from surgery. There wasn't any reason for me to stay there after that."

"Barb, I'm so sorry." The revelation that she'd been married to another woman was muted for me by her obvious grief.

"Don't be," she told me. "It was more than a year and a half ago. A big nasty mess it all was but it's done. I'm doing my best to try and move on, now. My...my parents are all I have left and my dad's health is bad. They need me. That's why I came back here."

"We have that in common. I mean, my father is long gone...not dead...just gone. I never really knew him but my mom has cancer. I don't think she has much longer. I came back to be here with her."

"That's sad. She can't be very old."

"Fifty-four."

"So where were you before you moved home?"

"Lovely Hancock County Indiana, with the Sheriff's Department there. I lived in Indy."

Recognition dawned in her eyes. "And I...we...Lisa and I, that is, owned a bar in Indy. Actually, a dance club. *That's* where we met!" she wagged a finger at me.

I studied her face for a split second and pointed back at her, incredulous, "The attempted rape case!"

She nodded vigorously. "Yes. Lisa and I took over that place and closed it down to remodel it completely. We'd been re-opened maybe two months with mostly new staff when that happened." She shuddered visibly. "That guy was a real dirt bag but now I remember meeting you. You were the cop that was there." She studied me now. Your hair was long then but shorter than it is now."

"And yours is longer now than it was then. You wore it pretty short."

We were both quiet but then a question niggled at me. "Whatever happened to that guy?"

"You don't know?"

"Nope. Marion County took over after I got the victims statement. I was never called in to court or anything."

"The deputies hauled him away in cuffs that night. He had the nerve to ask me to bail him out of jail or help him get a lawyer since he was being accused of something during his time on the clock. He tried to make it like it was our responsibility for him being scum."

"What did he get?"

"She didn't want to face him in court, Janet; she was so young. He pled out. I never saw him after I was subpoenaed to appear for the hearing and he was there."

"He didn't come back to work until his plea hearing?"

"Hell no," she told me half under her breath. "I fired him as they were hauling him out of the bar that night and made sure he heard me. That's why it was such a surprise that he wanted us to bail him out originally and pay for a lawyer."

Chapter 21

Janet
December 25ᵗʰ, 2014
The Crane Family Farm

Mel opened the door to find Barb standing there and offered by way of greeting, "Come on in! Glad you could make it." I didn't think she saw me standing off to one side.

"I hope it's okay;" Barb asked her, "I brought a friend?"

She stepped aside and I moved into view. Mel's pleased expression tightened just a little.

"If it's going to be a problem," I began.

"No, no; no problem for *me* anyway." Her smile spread again and I felt a little relief.

She stepped aside so we could enter and she took our jackets.

"I know where the kitchen is," Barb told her. "We come bearing gifts of food and wine." She wandered away leaving me standing there with my boss.

"I apologize," I stated quietly. "I knew this would be awkward for you."

"Not for the reason you think." As she responded, Dana joined us.

"Janet, what a surprise," she said and then turned and gave Mel a lopsided grin.

"Mom actually wanted Shane to come today too," Mel continued to me, mentioning the other department detective, "but he was going to see his family. I'm kind of surprised you're not with your mother." Her statement was more of a question.

"Since I'm on call, I can't really wander too far. Mom went with Aunt Leslie to their other sister's house which is on the other side of Columbus and, because of my chosen 'lifestyle' I'm not exactly welcome there anyway."

"Oh," Dana said, "that's a tough one but we sort of know how that goes. It's too bad you don't get to be with your mom today though."

"It's okay, we celebrated together last night."

"So, are you and Barb seeing each other?" Mel blurted out.

"Not in so many words," I responded carefully. "Not yet. We're just getting to know each other, I'd say."

"Barb's a friend," Mel told me. "She's had it pretty rough."

Dana shot her a look.

"What?" she asked her in return. "I'm just saying."

"It's okay, really," I replied. We're just friends for now. One day at a time."

Barb rejoined us. "So, she asked, "Are we cool? We're not stepping on any toes?"

"We're all cool," Mel told her as Dana nodded.

"What was your remark earlier?" Barb quizzed Mel, not quite ready to let it go. "You said it isn't a problem for *me*."

Dana rescued her, "Mel's mom still has a little trouble with the whole lesbian couple thing. She's coming around though."

"Yeah," Mel nodded as she spoke. "*Dana's* mother and her open mindedness are a big part of that. Those two have become fast friends. Chloe's easy going style seems to be rubbing off a little."

"So no PDA's or after dinner sex, got it," Barb joked just loud enough for the little group of us to hear. As we all laughed, another knock sounded at the door.

An older woman, who was just entering the room, called out, "I'll get it," and then, under her breath but just loud enough for the four of us to hear as she walked by us, "since no one else ever hears the door."

"Whoever you are, I hope you're hungry," she called in greeting as she pulled the door open and then stopped short.

Her face drained of color as she stepped back to reveal a cute, beaming young woman holding the hand of another pretty young woman.

Must be mother Crane, I thought to myself, as the older woman stood shell shocked.

Not noticing their hosts obvious distress, "Merry Christmas!" both women called out.

The four of us moved toward the door in a group to welcome the unsuspecting newcomers.

"That was quite an interesting afternoon," Barb said as we drove away from the party back toward her bar where I'd parked my own car.

"You're not kidding there. I thought Mrs. Crane was going to have heart failure." I smiled nervously and glanced at my pseudo date as she drove.

When she only shook her head in response, we fell into an uneasy silence but, fortunately, the trip was short.

As we pulled into the lot outside the Boar's Head, Barb finally spoke again. "Would you like a drink?"

"Here?" I was confused.

"Yes...I mean, it's just after 7:00. I planned to open at 8:00."

"Oh. I see. I guess I thought you'd be closed today."

She shrugged and replied, "I didn't expect to get into much today or to stay at Mel's folks as long as we did. I had Christmas with my parents last night and I took them over food this morning. I figured after the party today I'd be at loose ends and I could just open for anyone else that needed to get away from all of their own holiday hullabaloo too."

"I'm technically on duty...I'm on call."

"Coffee then?" Her new offer seemed a little halfhearted.

"No, not today," I said. "How about a rain check though some afternoon or evening when you don't need to be here?"

Barb nodded. "It's a deal. I'll give you a call." Her tone said otherwise.

We got out of her SUV and hugged briefly. I watched her as she walked toward the front door and let herself in. She sketched a slight wave at me as she closed the door behind her.

I didn't know what I felt and I didn't want to examine my feelings any closer.

Chapter 22

February 12th, 2015

I was just coming on shift when Mel beckoned to me. "You're with me," she said. "Let's go."

As we made our way to her vehicle she told me there was some sort of biker ruckus going on at the Boar's Head.

Her personal cell rang as we were climbing into her vehicle. "Barb," she said glancing at it before she answered it. "I just got the call," she answered her without preamble. "I'm enroute. Where are you?"

Barb's voice came through loud and clear as Mel's Bluetooth picked her up. "On my way there too. Almost there in fact; the alarm company called me."

"Turn around and go home. It's probably nothing."

"No way, Mel."

"I promise," she said back, "I'll call you as soon as I assess the situation."

Barb hung up without saying another word.

We arrived at the scene 15 minutes later to find more than a dozen motorcycles tearing around in the parking lot in the late winter cold and driving across the now broken up remnants of what had been the front entry porch. The door was standing wide open and the dark tinted glass front window was shattered. Inside we could see that there were more bikes and bikers.

Outside, one biker fired a shotgun into the air and hollered something but I couldn't make out what he was saying above the roar of all of his marauding fellow gangbangers on Harleys.

Three cruisers were already on the scene, amassed across the road. Barb's own SUV was over there too, several yards behind the three cruisers, but I couldn't see her inside.

Mel pulled in alongside the car of the Patrol Sergeant, Joe Treadway, and parked then got on her two way and ordered traffic diversions to be set up immediately in both directions and coming North out of Morelville.

After that, we both dismounted. Using our doors as shields, we worked our way around the back of the SUV and up behind Treadway's cruiser. He was back behind it, keeping it between him and the bikers across the way. He had his shotgun at the ready and a look of pure determination in his eyes.

"What the hell, now?" Mel questioned him.

"Other than they're all Z Renegades over there, no idea Sheriff. Been here about 10 minutes. Gates and McDonald both got here just before me. They said it was already like this when they got here."
Mel tossed her head backwards. "That's the owner's SUV back there. Where's she?"
"I told her to get back in it and get out of here. She's in there; won't leave."
She moved back over to her SUV, popped the rear lift gate and got out her own shotgun and handed it to me. Then she took out a portable bullhorn and a pair of binoculars. Moving back alongside Treadway, she raised the optics to her eyes and peered across at the bar.
A man across the street mounted a bike, fired it up and, holding a shotgun aloft, drove to the edge of the lot where he faced us. He idled the bike and hollered something across the road. I couldn't hear what he said.
Treadway raised his shotgun but Mel put out a hand to stay him as the biker turned and, still holding the gun, waved his arms at the other men on bikes. 'Juice' was stitched across the back of his jacket.
In ones and twos, the other bikers pulled up alongside him and idled their bikes too.

When it was quieter, Mel got on the bullhorn. "You must cease and desist now!"

Laughter peeled from the other side of the road. 'Juice' waved a hand for quiet. When his posse quieted down, he screamed across the divide, "You're outmanned and outgunned pigs; fall back! We're taking back our old hang out. I rule this turf now!"

He fired his bike back up and the others followed suit then. Driving out onto the road, he circled back to the bar. The other men all pulled or backed their rides away too and resumed the craziness of just a couple of minutes before.

"He's right," Mel said to those of us in earshot. "We are outmanned and outgunned, for now. We're sitting ducks over here if they decide to rush us."

The driver's side door to the SUV behind us swung open. We both turned to watch as Barb stepped down.

"Get back in your truck!" Mel yelled. She didn't listen to her. Marching right up to her, she screamed too, "My bar! Do something!" She grabbed Mel by the shoulders. Treadway and I both moved from opposite sides to pry her hands away from our boss.

"Don't hurt her," Mel cautioned us.

"Mel, you have to save my bar. My life...everything I have left...that's all of it. Besides my house, there isn't any more after fighting for Lisa's life and battling that damn hospital!"

It seemed like Mel zoned out for several long seconds, as if she was lost in a memory. Abruptly, she shook her head and stared hard across the street at the bar.

Still holding onto one of Barb's arms with one hand, I started to follow her gaze but she turned to me then, plucked the shotgun from my other hand and told me, "Take her truck and get her home."

I nodded.

"I'm not leaving!" Barb cried out.

"We've got this," Mel asserted back to her, "but it's not safe for you to be here right now. I can't do what I need to do if I'm worried about you." She stared into Barb's eyes and waited for her response. Finally, she relented. She shook herself loose of the grip Treadway still had on the other arm and turned toward her truck. Stopping me, Mel cautioned, "Stay with her and, whatever you do tread softly."

As we drove south, away from the bar, Barb was silent. She sat, half turned in the passenger seat, looking back until The Boar's Head slipped from view. Finally, she spun back around but she stared straight ahead, not really seeing, I felt, just lost inside her own thoughts.

"Mel will do everything in her power to get it back Barb; get it back *today*."

She didn't look at me as she responded, "If they leave anything for me to have back."

We drove the rest of the way to Morelville in silence. When I reached the edge of the village, I asked, "Can you tell me where we're going please?"

Barb pointed ahead. "Turn right at the next block."

I did as she said.

"It's the colonial half a mile down on the right."

Just outside of the village limits, there were no more homes until we came to Barb's colonial mini-mansion set a few acres back off the road. I tried to keep my surprise in check as I drove along the gravel track back to the house.

"You're thinking it's too big for just one person, aren't you?"

"No," I said. "I'm thinking it's beautiful."

"I shouldn't have bought it. It's too much to keep up for just me. Mom and dad are getting up there in years. I thought maybe they'd want to come here but they like the little one floor condo they have in Zanesville."

"Do you love it?"

Barb looked the house over. "I do," she answered. "I do."

"That's all that matters then."

Not knowing what to expect inside, I was surprised by the comfort that was evident even though the place was decorated simply with a mix of antiques and newer pieces designed for a modern country home.

"This is amazing Barb."

"You like it?"

"Absolutely. I guess I expected a lot of antiques and you do have some but, I don't know how to say it...I didn't expect the soft leather couch and chairs and all the wood. It looks so warm and comfortable."

"Dana's mother did most of it. She's quite talented."

"Chloe did this?" I spun around looking at everything again.

Barb nodded. "She did Mel and Dana's place and figured out she had a knack for it. I asked her to do mine."

"Where are my manners," she asked herself more than me. Can I get you something to drink?"

"No thank you. I'm fine."

Barb moved toward a sofa facing the fireplace in the great room and sat down heavily. I took a seat in a soft leather armchair a few feet from her and waited for whatever was coming next.

"Can I ask you a question?" I said to her, when the silence became unsettling.

She tilted her head to look at me and nodded her consent.

"Would you have come back here if your parents were...well?" I was certainly curious but, more than that, I wanted to get her mind off what was going on at her business.

She half smiled. "I grew up in Zanesville...couldn't wait to get out of town. A couple years after high school, I left. I went to live with an aunt out on the west coast. It was a whole different world, a whole different way of life. I loved it out there and...that's when I figured a few things out."

I just nodded and let her talk.

There were probably twenty different jobs and almost as many women along the way when I met Lisa and settled down. I'd finally finished college taking classes here and there at night. I had a business degree but no idea what to do with it.

Lisa had a background in hospitality and restaurant management. She got a little bit of money from an inheritance when we'd been together about seven or eight months. We used it to buy our first bar; a ramshackle old gay bar in a gay ghetto that was being 'gentrified'. We hung in there and sold it for what we thought then was a small fortune. We spent a little of it but reinvested most of the rest into another place."

"Over the years, we just kept moving from place to place rehabbing failing bars in good locations. We sold most of them but kept a few others for income. Everything was good until Lisa got...sick..."

Barb grew quiet. Her eyes became unfocused as she seemed lost in her thoughts. I felt bad about leading her down that track but I didn't know how to pull back now that she was on it.

A sob escaped from her throat and her arm shook as she raised her hand to her face and covered her eyes.

I stood and moved to the sofa where I took a seat beside her. Gently, I placed an arm around her shoulders and pulled her to lean against me as she sobbed.

"I'm so sorry," she choked out several long minutes later. "I think I've finally gotten a grip on it all and then it just comes back in a wave."

"It's okay Barb, really."

"I came back here because I realized I'd already lost everything but my parents that meant anything to me. I just can't bear to lose any more, you know? Not right now. Them, this house and that bar are all I have left." She looked at me intently.

My thoughts were a jumble as I nodded silently and then sucked in a deep breath. I knew I should get back to the scene and try and lend whatever help I could but I certainly didn't want to leave Barb alone in her current state.

I took my arm from around her and started to put a little distance between us on the sofa but she put a hand on my leg and stopped me cold.

"Thank you," she said simply, her eyes still rimmed with tears. "It's hard for me to open up about all of that."

"You're welcome," I responded back. It was all I could think of to say.

Barb held my gaze for several seconds and then leaned toward me, closing the distance between us. She brushed my lips with hers in a soft kiss that was completely unexpected. I froze. I didn't know how to take it or if I should respond. Taking advantage of a woman in a weak moment wasn't my style.

Barb's cell buzzing on the side table where she'd dropped it when we came in saved me.

She twisted around to grab it and said, "It's Dana," before she answered it.

I stood and stepped away to a window to look out and to give her a little privacy so I only got one side of the conversation but I heard her tell Dana that I was with her and that, yes, it was the bar.

She hung up after a minute or so and beckoned me back toward her. I moved back toward the center of the room but remained standing and kept a little distance between us.

"Dana said the local radio stations are all reporting about the bar. She called to see if I was all right. Morelville's on lockdown and they're all sitting around at Kris's house."

"Lockdown? Mel just wanted the roads blocked so nobody made it up to the intersection near the Boar's Head and got hurt. That's got to have people all freaked out."

Barb looked at me strangely.

"What?" I asked, when I finally noticed her watching me.

"You're antsy all of a sudden. Did I make you uncomfortable?"

I hadn't realized that I was bouncing from foot to foot. Self-consciously, I stopped. "No; it's not you. I'm just really thinking I should be up there helping them do whatever they're going to do to save your place but there's no way I'm leaving you by yourself."

"I appreciate that," she said, "but you need to do what you need to do. I'm a big girl."

"Nope; I'm not leaving you. I have my orders."

Barb nodded and appeared thoughtful. After a pause, she said to me, "How about you run me over to Kris's place? I know all of them. I'll just hang there and do whatever they're doing. You can take my truck back up to the bar."

###
February 16th, 2015
The Boar's Head

"I really appreciate you all coming to help me clean," Barb told the group of us that included Dana and her mother Chloe, Mel's

147

mother Faye and me, my mom and my aunt. "It's a disaster in here after the gang takeover but, thanks to Mel and her team, at least it's still standing. Mess we can deal with. Rubble, not so much."

"At least you're in good spirits about it," Chloe Rossi replied to her. "What do you want us to do?" Barb started telling our little group about the most pressing tasks. While she did that, I sort of edged away from my mom and more toward her so I could try and get a private word with her.

My mom was having one of her better days but she still wasn't very mobile. I was off for the day though and she wanted to spend it with me so here we were. When she was finally done handing out assignments, I pulled Barb aside and explained the situation.

Tipping my head toward mom, I told her, "If you could have her role silverware, or...or, well anything she could do sitting down. She wants to help but I can't let her overdo it." I glanced over at Aunt Leslie who, apparently figuring out what I was up to, was keeping my mom distracted.

"No problem Barb told me." With that, she turned sharply around and marched herself right over to mom. "Mrs. Mason," she addressed her, "do I have a job for you! How's your eye for detail?"

"It's just fine and call me Edith. What do you need from me dear?" My mom actually smiled, seemingly happy to be tasked with something.

"Those dirty bikers all but destroyed this place. Now, I've been able to put a lot of the furniture and such back to right and with this crew, we'll get most of the rest of the cleanup done today but I just don't have the time or the patience for some of the file sorting. They just trashed my office and my files. It would be great if you could help with any of that at all but you just tell me now, if you don't want to do it."

"I'll do whatever you need."

"You sit right there then. I'll be right back with some stuff to get you started." Barb turned to me and said, "Janet, if you don't mind, I'll need just a bit of a hand." She whirled and headed toward the kitchen while mom looked on. Not sure what I was about to get into, I followed somewhat more slowly than Barb was moving.

I found her in her office turning a key in a locked filing cabinet. "Grab an empty box from over there, if you would."

I picked up a box that had, at one time, held a dozen bottles of Kentucky bourbon and handed it to her. She plucked the bottle dividers out of it and laid them on her desk then set the box down on her chair. She pulled a dozen or more banded stacks of credit card receipts out of a cabinet drawer, un-banded them and started to throw the stacks into the box.

"Mix those up like tossed salad," she commanded.

I did as I was told while she dug out several more stacks; one for each day for at least a couple of weeks. As she handed them off to me, I mixed those in too.

These go with a shred company once a month but I keep them in here until they're picked up. Those hoodlums tried to get into the safe but they didn't bother with this cabinet.

"Thanks Barb. I appreciate this. Trying to sort through all of these out to keep her out of trouble and out of our hair for a while."

"I'm sorry," she said.

"Excuse me?"

"For not calling you. I...I... I don't even know where to start with you."

"How about we just start over again as friends for now, huh? Neither one of us is in any position for anything beyond that right now. You're still grieving and I get that. You also have a mess here on your hands and your own parents to think about and you saw out there what I'm dealing with."

She pursed her lips and nodded at me.

Chapter 23

Barb
Early Tuesday Afternoon, March 10ᵗʰ, 2015

"Hey Mel, what's up?"

"Edith Mason was admitted to Genesis late last night. It doesn't look good...I just thought you'd want to know."

"Oh my. How's...how's Janet doing?"

"About as well as can be expected, under the circumstances. She's with her now."

"Yeah...okay. Thanks for letting me know."

I hadn't set foot in a hospital since the day Lisa died. Other than running dad to appointments with various doctors, I hadn't had anything at all to do with the medical profession since then either. Just the thought of entering a healthcare facility to visit a patient in the last stages of life unnerved me.

'Janet's your friend; you have to go,' my brain and my heart told me. In my soul, I wasn't so sure.

It had been years since I'd been inside the Genesis facility. When I inquired at the information desk for Edith's room number, I was directed to the trauma unit. That both puzzled and scared me.

Following the signs along the main floor toward ER, I found the trauma area pretty easily even though much of the building had been renovated and redesigned since I'd last been in it. When I stopped at the locked double doors leading to the patient area, my heart was pumping so hard, it felt like it was going to come out of my chest. Trying to calm myself just a little, I took a couple of deep breaths and then buzzed to be let back into the unit.

Edith's room was directly across from the nurse's station. Janet was standing facing the door when I walked up to it. There was no turning back now.

It wasn't until I got into the room that I realized Edith's sister Leslie was also there. She was bent over the bed on the side nearer the door but out of direct view, speaking in a low tone directly into her sister's left ear. Edith lay on her back on the bed, her eyes closed, her features gaunt, an oxygen cannula in her nose. Though she wasn't hooked up to any other monitors, she looked to be barely clinging to life.

Leslie turned toward the sound of my footsteps, pursed her lips into a thin line and slightly shook her head. I got the message; the prognosis wasn't good. She turned back to her sister and I walked toward Janet.

"You didn't have to come," she said.

"It's the least I could do; after the things you've done for me."

Janet sighed. "She was a little out of it and in a lot of pain when we brought her in but conscious and able to communicate. For the last

152

three hours she's been completely non-responsive."

"What are they thinking...I mean, what are they planning to do?"

Janet was silent. It was Leslie who answered my question. "There's nothing they can do, dear."

Janet whispered, "This is it. It's the end."

My heart dropped. I shook my head and whispered, "I'm so sorry."

Shortly after my arrival, Genesis moved Edith from Trauma to the hospice area. I stayed throughout the day to support Janet and Leslie and to act as a go-fer for whatever they needed. Several times I stepped out of Edith's room to make way for various family members and friends that came in a thin trickle throughout the day to make a final call to the barely living woman.

At one point Janet joined me in the family waiting area. I was just stirring sugar into a cup of coffee when she rounded the corner of the hallway and entered the room.

"Taking a break?"

She nodded.

"Coffee?"

She nodded again then leaned back against the counter as I made her a cup.

"My Aunt Rhoda showed up, mom's other sister."

"The one that's 'holier than thou'?"

"That's the one."

I shot her a look.

"Really, I tried to be nice; bit my tongue several times as she was barking out questions and orders. It just got to be too much. I had to leave before I said or did something I'd regret."

"Good for you. How long do you think she'll be here; I mean, you can't hide out forever."

"Not very long, I'd imagine. I'm sure she has far more important things to do today than sit here all day."

"Is she really that bad?"

Janet just looked at me.

Much later, well after the dinner hour, it was just the four of us there in the room again. Edith was still hanging on to a thin strand of life but she hadn't moved a muscle or so much as flicked an eyelid in response to someone speaking to her in hours. Death was imminent.

"You need to go home Aunt Leslie. Get some rest."

She looked at her husband Bob who'd arrived after a long day of tending to their family farm and their animals solo to pay his own respects and to try and coax his wife home. "I just can't leave her," she told him.

"You've been here for hours," Janet said. "She doesn't even know we're here anymore, any of us. There isn't anything else we can do now but wait. I can do that. You go home, sleep and come back in the morning."

"But, what if she passes in the night?"

I stepped in then, "Then you and Janet will need to get together to make funeral arrangements. You'll need to be fresh and thinking clearly for that." Bob nodded his agreement and coaxed her to say her goodbyes.

Finally, after a round of whispering in her sisters' ear and hugs for all of us, Bob ushered her out the door. Janet and I were quiet. I watched her and she watched her mother.

Around midnight, as I stood to stretch my aching muscles, I could have sworn Edith moved just a little. I watched her intently. Janet was half dozed off, sitting straight up in a chair. I wasn't about to disturb her if I was simply seeing things in my own tired state of mind.

Scooting my chair a foot or so closer to the bed, I perched on the edge and watched her face. Her eyes flickered; not open but there was movement. Then, they did it again. I stood and moved to her.

"Edith, it's Barb. Can you hear me?"

Janet jerked awake. "What are you doing?" she called to me even though I was barely three feet from her.

"I swore I saw her sort of shudder a minute ago and now her eyes are flickering."

"How is that possible? Do you think she's coming to?"

I shrugged. "I don't know. We should probably call for the nurse."

"This is called the 'fish out of water' stage; it's one of the last stages before death." we were informed in gentle tones. "You might want to say your final goodbyes now."

"She can hear me?" Janet asked.

The nurse nodded. "We think so. Do you want me to call her sister for you?"

"How much time do you think we have?"

"It could be minutes hon; it could be an hour or so."

"That fast?" Janet chocked out.

"Yes, unfortunately."

"No. Thank you though. I'll call her in the morning. She needs to rest."

"That's fine. I'll just step out and page the on-call doctor."

At 12:37 AM, Wednesday, March 11th, 2015 my most recently made friend, Edith Mason passed on. Her daughter Janet, all but completely estranged from her mother for most of the previous nine years, wept and I wept for her and for myself; the sting of loss cutting through me again like a knife.

Chapter 24

Janet had ridden to the hospital in the squad that she'd called to come for her mother. Leslie's car was still in the nearly vacant visitor parking lot since, exhausted, she'd ridden home with Bob but Janet didn't have a key for it. I couldn't, in good conscience, leave her to fend for herself anyway, even if she had, had access to the car.

After bundling her into my own vehicle in the coolness of the night and getting the address to her family home since I'd never been there, we were off. We rode in silence, Janet lost in her misery and me reliving my own pain of loss and the depression that followed it.

"This is it, right here." They were the only words she'd spoken in more than ten minutes. She pointed to a craftsman style bungalow on the right side of a residential street in an older Zanesville neighborhood.

Two cars filled the tiny driveway that led back to a single car garage set apart from the house. I pulled my SUV into any empty space along the curb in front and parked. Janet didn't move; she just stared out at the house.

"Do you want me to go inside with you? Would that help?"

"Yes," came in response and then she opened the door and slid down out of the seat. I turned and did the same. By the time I made it around to the other side of the truck, she was standing upright and fumbling in her coat pocket for something but she hadn't moved otherwise.

When she finally pulled out a set of keys, she looked first at me and then proceeded down the driveway to a side door.

We entered through the kitchen. Janet moved far enough inside for me to get in myself and get the door closed but she seemed hesitant to go any further. Not knowing what else to do, I moved in behind her and embraced her. She sank back against me and we just stood like that for several long seconds.

She was taller than me by a few inches. Tilting my chin up after a minute or so, I told her, I'll stay as long as you need me but, honestly, you need rest."

Janet looked back at me and gave me the slightest smile. She turned then and I loosened my hold just a little to allow her to do so.

Once we were face to face, she said to me, "Thanks...for everything, for...for..."

"Shh. It's okay. You'd do the same for me."

She looped her arms around me then and pulled me in for a hug. I don't know how long we stood there like that as first she rocked us gently and then she shuddered, stopped rocking and clung tightly as she broke down into sobs.

I just let her cry. Eventually I cried along with her in sympathy with her own pain now. For the first time in a couple of years, my thoughts weren't on my own loss but on the needs of someone else.

Janet eventually tried to pull back but I wouldn't let her go all the way; not yet.

"I'm sorry," she said. "Look at me blubbering like a baby." She let go of me with one hand and raised her arm to dab at her eyes with her sleeve.

I let go with a hand too and, after brushing my own eyes with two fingers, I ran the back of my hand down the tear trail of her cheek. She pulled me in then and kissed me, softly, on the nose.

I raised my chin at the tickle her kiss gave me and, quite by chance, our lips brushed. This kiss was far more hesitant and ever so gentle.

Almost as if drawn by some gravity between us, our lips pressed together a little harder. Through the grief, a subtle note of pleasure was added.

Janet's tongue gently caressed my lip and I trembled wondering; do I respond? Part of me wanted to, desiring that intimacy and the sensuality of connection. Another part of me didn't want to take advantage of a woman who might only be acting in the throes of her grief. Thoughts of Lisa though didn't even cross my mind. My focus was only in the present.

Without a word, Janet reached to me and, slipping her hand behind my head, she pulled me up to her into a kiss that it seemed later, when I recalled it, had been too long in coming.

Like before, the touch of our lips was gentle at first but then grew harder. This time, though I hesitated when her mouth opened, I didn't pull away.

Giving in finally, my own lips opened slightly as our kiss deepened and I feel the brush of her tongue. That was all it took for me to give myself fully to the kiss as I tangled a hand in her long blond hair.

We laid side by side, naked and slightly chilled at first in the initial coolness of her sheets. I could feel her body heat but we weren't touching, not yet. As Janet pulled her comforter over us, I reached across to her to move a lock of hair off her face.

She reached out to me then too and let her hand caresses my hip and thigh. I closed my eyes and responded by gently running my hand over her shoulder and down her back. The feel of her skin, so soft and so smooth, was wonderful. Her warm breath flowed across my lips just before our mouths connected. This time our kiss was deeper, leaving me panting, wanting more.

My body responded. My nipples grew tight and hard and so did Janet's. The feeling when we rubbed together was so intense, I immediately felt hot and wet at my center. I could feel swelling and slick, slippery wetness as I moved my legs to adjust my position and press closer against her.

Her hand slid up and she gently stroked my breast. I couldn't help the sigh that wrenched out of me at the pleasure of her touch.

My response encouraged her and she brushed a thumb back and forth across my already hardened nipple. The feeling was so fantastic, I cried out.

She went further then, squeezing the nipple and rolling it between her fingers. I ran my hand lower from the curve of her waist until I felt the swell of her bottom and couldn't resist squeezing it. Her skin there was smooth too but she was firm and toned.

She bent her head then and another new sensation from my breast and nipple sent exquisite tingles though me as her warm, wet tongue circling my aureole and nipple.

Janet pushed me gently from my side onto my back where she straddled me while she continued to suckle. The feeling of her weight on me, of our skin touching and what her mouth was doing to me set every nerve ending in my body on fire.

As I writhed beneath her, she started to move down my body. The comforter that had been tented over her shoulders now moved down with her, leaving me exposed, naked on her bed.

I gasped as a feathery kiss was placed at the top of my little strip of pubic hair. I looked down and watched as she rose up to her knees, the comforter falling away from her, the single bedside lamp illuminating her toned, beautiful body. Her breasts were firm and smooth atop a stomach with abs defined by exercise I didn't even know she did. There was, I realized then, so little I really knew about her.

My eyes travelled further down to see that her own hair was trimmed in a neat, narrow 'V' shape that terminated just above her cleft. I admired her longingly, wantonly.

Her hands caressed my thighs as she looked down at me while I gazed up at her.

"I want to make love to you Barb," said simply. I nodded, too excited to speak or to think beyond the moment.

She started stroking the inside of my thighs and my legs parted of their own accord. Whatever anxieties were playing in my mind, my body seemed to have decided on what it wanted on its own.

Her fingers slipped through the dampness of my little strip of pubic hair and ever so softly traced the line of my swollen inner lips. She parted my nether lips and worked her fingers through my folds, sliding them gently up and down.

I raised my hips, forcing her deeper. The feeling was incredible. It had been so long since I'd been made love to, I couldn't get enough. I begged her to enter me and, when she did, gently moved my hips in time with her thrusts, the excitement building inside me.

Her fingers withdrew all too soon and my eyes flicked open to see was happening. Janet looked me in the eye as she raised her fingers to her mouth and sucked them, her eyes closing as she savored the taste of my juices coating them.

"Barb, you taste so good," she told me as she lowered herself. I heard her inhale, smelling the musky scent of my arousal before her exhaled breath glided over my folds. I caught myself biting my lip in anxious anticipation. The first gentle lap of her tongue brought both intense pleasure and the nagging pain of my engorged clit, begging for attention and release.

Her tongue licked and probed, caressed and tasted. I was soon writhing on the bed again as my climax built within me and yet her mouth seemed to keep finding new ways to stimulate me.

She gave my throbbing clit tiny little laps and then slid her fingers once again into my hot, dripping core. I was so close to the edge then, my gasps and moans increased in volume and tempo.

Her fingers and her mouth switched places then; her tongue probing deeply while her fingers strummed away on my throbbing clit.

I bucked and my muscles spasmed with the climax that rocketed through me. Her mouth and fingers kept playing me, stretching my orgasm beyond anything I could rightly recall. Finally, with a last gasping sigh, I flopped back onto her bed, dizzy, exhausted, spent and tingling in the aftermath.

Janet crawled up to lie beside me pulling the comforter along with her and over us as she put her arm across me.

I kissed her then. I could smell and taste myself on her mouth. I could not possibly deny the passion and arousal I felt for her. I didn't want to.

Without a word between us, we both drifted off to sleep.

Chapter 25

Janet
Some Time After 5:00 AM, Wednesday, March
11ᵗʰ, 2015
Mason Family Home

I did it again! I was sitting in the living room on the sofa, my knees drawn up to my chest, only a thin blanket wrapped around me. I felt like I should suffer in the morning chill of late winter.

It was evident in my mind that I'd made a terrible mistake with Barb. Now, I thought to myself, another woman who really had no feelings for me would be completely distancing herself from me. I hugged the blanket in close and rocked myself, trying to will away the memory and the pain that was sure to come with the dawn.

At some point, sleep overcame me again and I curled into a fetal ball on the couch. That's where Barb found me later. She was wearing an old bath robe that I never used but for some reason left hanging on the back of my door and, it appeared, nothing much else.

"Why are you out here? I didn't push you from your own bed did I?" she asked.

"No. I couldn't sleep...at least...not very long. I'm used to being up early, I guess. I just sat here for a while. I must have drifted off."

"Oh."

That was all she said. I tried for polite. "Do you want some coffee?"

"No thank you. I'm fine."

She was being polite too.

"If you don't mind though, do you have a pair of sweatpants or something like that and a T-shirt I could borrow? I'll certainly return them."

Of course, I thought. She wants to leave. Her dress clothes from the day before were strewn across the living floor. I looked over them with an intense pang of guilt. "I'll just be a minute," I told her.

I went into the bathroom first and splashed my face with frigid water. With the cold came clarity and I knew that no matter what I felt for this woman, I couldn't divulge those feelings to her. I didn't want to drive her away and lose her completely like I had Gevona. Being casual friends with Barb would be better than heartbreak and the total loss of any sort of connection to her at all.

Dressing quickly, I picked some things out that I thought might fit her and carried them out to her. While I was gone, she'd collected her own clothes and folded them neatly. She was setting the little pile of them on the corner of the kitchen table nearest the side door when I walked into the room.

"Here you go. The pants might be a little long," I said as I held the clothes out to her.

"Thanks," her cheeks tinted slightly red, "I'll just be a minute. Though I'd seen her in all her glory just a few hours before, she retreated down the hall toward the bathroom.

Before Barb could return to the kitchen, a knock sounded at the front door. I trudged through the living room, released the bolt and pulled it open to find Mel and Dana on the front porch. They were loaded down with bags and Mel was toting a box as well. Puzzled but stepping aside, I invited them in.

"What on earth are you two doing here? And, shouldn't you be at work?" I addressed my uniformed boss.

"First of all, our condolences," Dana offered. "We're both really sorry for your loss." Mel nodded to punctuate her wife's statement.

"Thank you." I didn't know what else to say.

"Now then, we're here to see after you," Dana went on. "We come bearing food and coffee for one thing and, though Mel will have to leave shortly, I'm here to help you and your aunt with whatever you need today."

"Don't be surprised," Mel added, "if my mother and Dana's don't both show up to lend a hand with arrangements and such or whatever you might need as well."

"They don't have to do that. You've already done too much with this." I swung my arm to indicate the stuff they were still holding.

"Oh wait," Dana said. "If Zanesville is anything like McKeesport where I grew up, you're going to have people showing up in droves bearing food and sympathy. Let's get this stuff put away while there's still space available."

At that remark I smiled but the smile was short lived as Barb emerged from the bedroom hallway just as we three moved toward the kitchen.

"I thought I heard voices out here. Mel, Dana; good to see you. I wish it could be under better circumstances."

Jumping in quickly, I told them, "Barb stayed with me at the hospital until mom passed last night and then brought me home since I didn't have a way back here so late." My words tumbled out in a rush as Dana looked from me to her and back again.

"You could have just called the station, you know," Mel said.

"It's okay," Barb said. "She didn't need to be alone last night anyway. I'm afraid she didn't sleep well, regardless." She addressed all of that to the two of them as if I wasn't even there. Dana looked at me again and then turned back and studied her.

She knows what really happened; that I screwed up, I thought. "Did you say there was coffee?" I was grasping for straws now.

"Yeah, sure," Mel answered. She seemed oblivious to my real plight. "There's three cups in the box there. You three go ahead. I'm really not much of a coffee drinker anyway."

The phone rang just as I reached for the box. Excusing myself, I answered it instead and spent the next couple of minutes filling Aunt Leslie and Uncle Bob in while Barb, Dana and Mel made small talk.

When I hung up, I said to the group of them, "That was my aunt. She'll be here in about twenty minutes. We're going to work on funeral arrangements." I looked at Mel, "I'm going to need a little time off, uh, Sheriff."

She shook her head hard, "Of course you are. I wouldn't dream of having you come in to work right now. We can handle it for the rest of this week. You do what you need to do. If you need more time than that, just let me know."

"Thank you. I appreciate that."

Chapter 26

Dana Rossi-Crane
Saturday, March 14ᵗʰ, 2015

The viewing and funeral were held at Edith's church. Mel and I waited in line between rows of pews for several minutes before we reached the bier and the little cache of actual blood relatives Edith Mason had left.

Janet, standing closest to the casket, was holding up about as well as could be expected, better even than under the circumstances I'd found her in on Wednesday morning. Leslie was right by her side today which, I thought, was giving her some measure of comfort. She seemed to be close to her aunt.

"Dana, Mel, this is my Aunt Rhoda; my mother's other sister," Janet introduced us. "Aunt Rhoda, Dana helped with a lot of the arrangements for today and Mel is actually my boss; Sheriff Melissa Crane."

Rhoda eyed me and then Mel. Addressing my wife, she asked, "You use Mel? It seems so masculine."

Mel just gave her a tight lipped grin and we moved on but, out of the corner of my eye, I saw Leslie shoot her sister a quick 'be nice' sort of look.

Finding seats a few rows back, we sat but not before I caught sight of Barb entering the church. She was properly dressed in an understated black pantsuit for a funeral, yet she was strikingly beautiful with just a hint of jewelry and makeup on, something I'd rarely seen from her. More than one set of male eyes traveled her way, I noticed.

As I got settled, I watched the receiving line proceeding toward the front. Over the shoulder of one mourner, Janet looked out at the line in Barb's direction. She quickly looked away and focused back on the people directly in front of her.

There was some sort of issue between those two but I didn't know what was going on. I'd felt the tension in the room on Wednesday morning but that wasn't the time or the place for me to ask nosy questions. Barb left when Mel did that morning which was to say, she didn't stay more than a few minutes after we arrived.

When I mentioned what I sensed to Mel later, she swore she hadn't noticed anything amiss. She told me Janet was grieving and that probably brought up similar feelings again for Barb too so they were both probably feeling 'down' as she put it, and then she changed the subject so I let it drop.

After this funeral and a proper period of mourning for Janet, I'm going to get to the bottom of that, I vowed to myself.

A few minutes passed along with Mel and I studying the little programs for the service that we'd been given at the door when I looked up again to catch Leslie staring at the profile of a man standing at the bier. Janet was stealing quick looks at Barb who was waiting for her turn a few people behind him.

The man turned from viewing Edith's countenance, took a step toward Janet and reached out to take her hand. He was speaking but I couldn't make out the words. Whatever he was saying, she shrank away from him and tried to pull her hand away but he wouldn't let go. Leslie stepped sideways to face the two of them, her back to the room, cutting off my view of his face and Janet's. Her stance was rigid suggesting this mourner might be unwelcome.

I nudged Mel and told her what was going on. We both watched up front while the discussion proceeded for another thirty seconds or so and then Leslie stepped aside and the man left the receiving line, ignoring the curious looks of Aunt Rhoda who'd been shielded from and shut out of their conversation by Leslie.

He proceeded down the side aisle and, as I turned to follow his movement, he went all the way to the back of the sanctuary and out the front doors of the church. When I turned back around, Janet wasn't up front anymore, only Leslie and Rhoda were. Another man was speaking with them and Barb was at the bier. A few people remained behind her.

"What time is it?"

Mel consulted her watch. "1:20."

"I'm worried about Janet. Whoever that man was, it seems to have affected her. She's stepped away and there are still people in line for the viewing."

"The service starts soon. Maybe she needed a breather."

"I'm going to go and check on her."

Without waiting for a response, I got up and approached Leslie who was now greeting Barb.

"I'm sorry to interrupt but I saw that Janet left and I was concerned. Barb looked on, her features clouded, as I asked after the other woman. I just couldn't read her but I really didn't have time for that at the moment.

"She was taken by surprise and I'm worried that she may be more than just a little upset," Leslie confided. "Her father showed up. She hasn't seen him in 25 years or more and I guarantee she didn't remember him."

"Where'd she go?"

"Into the pastor's office; through there," she pointed, "and down the hall."

"I'll go check on her."

"Janet?" I tapped on the frosted glass upper portion of the closed door.

"It's open," she called out in a small voice.

Not knowing if the pastor was with her or not, I didn't say anything at first as I entered. When I didn't see him, only her sitting in one of the arm chairs around a small table at one side of the office, her elbows on the table, her head in her hands, I approached her speaking softly.

"Janet, honey, I came back here to check on you. Leslie told me what happened."

Moving behind her, I braced my hands on her shoulders and leaned in as she leaned back until we were hugging cheek to cheek. Her face was hot and she was trembling but not crying.

"Why did he wait and pick today of all days to show back up in my life and then try to introduce himself as my dad?"

It was a rhetorical question asked in anger. Knowing she needed to get it out, I stayed quiet and let her rant.

"He's not my 'dad'. He never was. He left my mom and me to fend for ourselves when I was barely four. She divorced him by mail after trying for years and years to even find him."

"Said he's been back in town for a while and wanted to contact us but he was afraid of what I might think of him. Ha! He got that right! Paying his respects, my ass!" She smacked a hand down on the table. "Where was all that 'respect' before?"

With that, she seemed to run out of steam. She exhaled loudly and dropped her head down.

"He left Janet. He's gone," I told her as I let go of her shoulders and took the chair adjacent to her.

"Only because Aunt Leslie got in his face and made sure he knew he wasn't welcome here."

"And hopefully," I said, "that will be enough to make him realize that he needs to give you plenty of time and space. It's your decision going forward whether to see him or not and only yours. And, frankly, it's not one you need to make now or any time soon."

"I don't even need to think about it at all, Dana. I'm not interested in getting to know him now or ever. He's a sperm donor, nothing more."

"Okay." I nodded at her. "That's fine." I didn't necessarily agree with her rash decision but I again found myself in a position of it not being the time or the place for my own opinions or questions. "Just push all of that out of your mind for now. There are other things we need to try and focus on today."

She sighed. "I know. You're right. I just need to pull myself together and get back out there for my mom and for my aunt."

I didn't bother to correct her. I knew she was thinking only of Leslie and not about her Aunt Rhoda.

When I got back to the pew, Barb was sitting next to Mel. She scooted down a little so I could sit between them. I gave her a little smile and she returned it but her focus turned quickly away from me as Janet re-entered the sanctuary.

For her part, Janet didn't even look around. She went right to Leslie and Rhoda who were receiving the last of the mourners up front. Shortly afterward the three of them took seats in the front pew and the pastor of the church began the memorial service.

Janet never turned around at all during the next thirty minutes or so. She sat nearly completely still through the entire service. Meanwhile, Barb spent most of the service staring at the back of her head.

Ethel Mason's three surviving family members and their spouses left the church with the casket for a private graveside service while the rest of us trundled downstairs to the fellowship hall for the wake. There, the somberness of the service upstairs was replaced with a mountain of food, conversation and laughter.

Mel, Barb and I each took loaded plates from the buffet line staffed by church members and found seats at one end of a long row of tables. Mel and I, as is typical of the two of us when we can manage it, given our backgrounds, chose positions at one end of the room facing the most used entry and exit door. Barb sat across from us with her back to it.

The conversations swirling all around quieted enough to be noticeable to Barb when Janet and her aunts and uncles returned to the church and entered the hall. She turned and locked eyes with Janet. Both women held their gaze for only a second or so and then broke off, Barb by turning back to us and Janet by looking at her feet.

As the group of five took plates and were served food, their backs to the room, I caught Barb stealing glances toward them again.

Something happened between these two, something they can't or won't face kept running through my head. When Mel asked Barb a question and she didn't respond because she was lost, off in her own thoughts, I decided now was better than later to do a little damage control. I just had to figure out how to get Barb alone and do a proper intervention.

In a marvelous stroke of luck, Shane Harding, Mel's other detective in the department, walked into the fellowship hall, found Janet and offered his condolences. He was introduced around and then directed to the serving line after which, Mel waved him over to our table.

"I didn't think I was going to make it over here at all," he told his boss as he took the offered seat. I got called out on a hit and run. I'd really wanted to be here at least for the viewing."

"Hit and run?" Barb asked him. "Everyone's okay, I hope?"

Shane shook his head. "No, unfortunately, but alive and likely to survive it."

I shuddered and played it up a bit. "Ouch. On that, I just need to step out for a minute and I'm sure Mel wants to quiz you a little more," I said to Shane.

Mel shrugged but I pressed on, "Barb, I'd love it if you'd join me."

"Hmm." I looked Barb up and down. We were outside where the air was cool but not cold. I hadn't grabbed my coat but I was comfortable.

"Hmm what? Something I should know?"

"I'm trying to decide between the direct approach or the circular one we use in interrogations."

"About what?" Her tone was more cautious than curious.

"Okay, direct it is. What's the problem between you two?"

"I beg your pardon?"

"Between you and Janet."

"What are you talking about? There's no problem. We're friends." Her tone wasn't very convincing.

"Just friends?"

Barb nodded but her rising color told me what I really needed to know. I paused for a few beats then switched to the circular approach.

"You look very nice today. I love the necklace."

"Really? Thanks." She touched the colored stone hanging at the base of her neck. "I've had it for ages, I just haven't felt like wearing jewelry in a while." She seemed relieved that I'd dropped the earlier line of questioning. "Funny, I didn't take you for a jewelry type."

178

"I'm not," I said, "but you look stunning today with it. Not that you don't always look nice but I don't recall that I've ever seen you wear much if any makeup either."

The color made it all the way to her cheeks now. "It's...it's sort of a formal occasion."

I nodded. "True, true." It was like manipulating a school girl instead of a 36-year-old woman.

I feigned feeling the pockets of my own suit jacket. "Crap! I left my cell phone inside. Do you have the time?" I knew she always wore a wrist watch. Cops and bar owners; they could all be counted on to know the exact time.

She raised her left arm and, after slipping her jacket and blouse sleeves back slightly to check, she reported, "It's 2:36."

Catching her arm before she could lower it again, I looked pointedly at her left hand. "No wedding band today though?"

Barb tried to pull her hand away but I held it and rubbed it gently.

"I don't know what happened between the two of you Tuesday night but I can guess. Are you okay?" My concern was genuine and I hoped it showed.

She nodded and stopped fighting my grasp.

"And how is Janet?"

"I think she regrets all of it."

"But you don't know that for sure?"

"I can feel it."

"Odd, because I'm getting a completely different vibe from her." I bounced our linked hands a couple of times. "Sweetie, look, you've obviously progressed far enough through the grieving process over Lisa that you're starting to heal and to take at least a little interest in living again. That's okay. You're allowed to come out the other end of all of that and enjoy life again."

She sucked in a deep breath and let it out real slow but she didn't say a word. I turned to face her and took her other hand up as well.

"It's also okay to let another woman into your heart that you obviously have feelings for."

"I'm scared Dana." She looked away, over my shoulder.

"I know; it's natural, but you can do this."

"It's not that...well, it's a little bit of that but even more: I'm not so sure what Janet wants or needs. She's in pain right now and I don't want to push her into something that's just a balm for that."

Chapter 27

Dana Rossi-Crane
3:12 PM, Saturday, March 14ᵗʰ 2016

"You were quiet the whole way home. What's going through that devious mind of yours?"

I swatted lightly at Mel's shoulder as she peeled her jacket off and then hung it on the back of a kitchen chair. "That's so wrong. You can't just go around making accusations like that."

"It was a question and, yes I can and I did." She opened the fridge, reached in and took out a diet Pepsi and held it out to me. I took it and waited while she got another one for herself.

"Barb and Janet slept together Tuesday night."

Mel jammed her thumb down into her can as she tried to pop the top of her soda. "Oww!"

"Sorry. Did you get cut?"

She removed the thumb carefully and flexed it. "No, but are there any more bombshells you want to drop before I try to do anything else?"

"I'm being serious. I told you it was tense when we were there Wednesday morning. They're not sure where they stand with each other but neither one of them wants to tell the other what she's feeling."

"They told you this?" She tossed that over her shoulder as she headed for the living room and her big leather recliner.

"Well, not both of them," I said following behind her. "Barb actually did but Janet's just an open book. Her feelings for Barb are written all over her face except Barb's the only one that can't see them. She thinks Janet's just grieving."

"She is; for her mother."

"Which is way different than for a lost love."

"Baby, we don't know what other kind of baggage she's dragging around."

"True. Could you talk to her? I mean, you're a lot closer to her than I am." I looked at my wife hopefully.

"Are you out of your mind? She's my employee. I'm not going to have a conversation with her about anything of the sort."

"I don't know what to do then. Those two belong together." I stared at her from my perch on the edge of the couch but she didn't flinch. You seriously won't help me get them together?"

"I didn't say that but...Dana, seriously, we should just let nature take its course. We both have a million other things to do and they're grown women. If they're meant to be together it'll happen."

"There's an obvious attraction there; a connection. I felt the electricity between them that night they met in Barb's bar. It's been simmering long enough; sometimes nature just needs a little help."

"Does it really matter what I say? You're going to plot something out anyway and, though I absolutely hate to admit it, it'll probably work."

I glossed over her dig about what she says not mattering to me and moved on to the greater point, "Yes, I'm going to make it my mission to get them together. If you won't help me then I'll just have to pull Mama in. She loves Barb so I know she'll help."

Mel laughed. "Well, we all know what will happen when you add the steamroller known as Chloe to the equation."

"What's that supposed to mean?"

"Nothing derogatory Dana, it's just that your Mama won't stop at anything she starts until she gets what she wants."

I could only nod. I had to agree with that.

Mel turned the TV on and started flipping channels. Meanwhile I started flipping through things in my mind, trying to formulate a plan.

While she watched a sitcom, I pretended interest but I was really plotting out a way to get my two friends together.

At a commercial break, when I felt Mel's eyes on me, I knew she was onto me. Instead of playing it off I just came right out and asked, "Just between you and me, "What's Janet's schedule looking like over the next week or so?"

Mel smirked. "I can't tell you that. Its confidential information."

"Oh, is that right? Mel Crane, do I have to beat it out of you?"

She let out a loud laugh "As if!" she replied but then her expression softened. "She's still on paid bereavement leave all this week, you know? I Imagine she'll need a few more days beyond today. She's got a lot she's got to do as the immediate next of kin. Leslie mentioned that Janet was thinking about selling that house. She doesn't like being right in Zanesville."

Hmm, interesting, I thought. To Mel I said, "Thank you. Was that so hard?"

Mel fell asleep in her chair.

Seeing my chance to act without any ribbing from the sidelines, I grabbed my wallet and my keys and headed over to the general store my parents ran in the village. I figured Mama and Dad would both be there since it wasn't a particularly nice March day. Dad would have no excuse to go off fishing with Mel's dad.

I was right. Mama was waiting on a customer at the register and Dad was sitting on the bench inside the store under one of the front windows, shooting the breeze with the man while he waited to be rung out.

There wasn't anyone else in the little store so I waited until their only customer was gone and then I asked, "Slow day?"

"Very; for a Saturday," Mama said. "This darn weather. A couple of hours ago it wasn't bad out now it's getting windy and chilly. Oh, but I'm sure you didn't come over here to talk about the weather. Did you go to that funeral?"

"Yeah, Mel and me both. So sad." I shook my head for effect.

"How's she doing; Janet, is it?"

"Yes. She's taking it all about as well as can be expected but she's sort of the reason I came to see you. I, uh, need a little help with something."

"Oh boy, I know that tone," my dad said. "Should I leave the room?"

"Oh Marco!" Mama swatted a hand in his general direction. "She could be about to ask about anything at all for goodness sake."

He laughed as Mel had before him. "Not likely. I'll just go to the back. Holler if you need me." With that he retreated into the office and closed the door.

"I'm afraid your father thinks he knows everything."

"In this case Mama, he's right. I need your help with a little plan to get two people together."

"Playing cupid are we?" She rubbed her hands together briskly, "You know how much I love that!"

"Do I ever. This time, instead of practicing on me and Mel, you get to practice on Barb, um sort of and, to top it off, you get to put your decorating and organizing talents to use."

"I'm liking the sounds of this. Go on..."

#

Mama went to church with Faye on Sunday but begged off the usual Sunday dinner at the Crane farm saying she'd promised to help a friend. It wasn't a lie, per se. She knew Janet and she was going to offer her assistance as a promise to me. Faye had her moments when she seemed to be coming around but, if she knew what the real plan was, she might have been more disapproving than supportive.

Once we reached Janet's house in Zanesville, I tried to quiz her one last time, "You remember the plan right?"

"Isn't this the cutest little place? Craftsman, isn't it? I could have so much fun with this."

"It's already pretty nice inside Mama. Mrs. Mason had some period pieces that she probably bought when she and...well, when they bought the house years ago."

"Really? Well now isn't that something?"

"Mama, just remember what I told you. Janet's told people she wants to sell. We're going to upsell you helping her to pack and get it ready for market, not redecorating it, okay?"

"Gotcha, staging."

"Right, whatever; let's go."

"We just came by to see how you were doing," I lied.

"Fine. I'm fine. Come in."

"I hope you don't mind, I brought Mama along."

"No, not at all. Chloe it's nice to see you again."

"You have my sympathy dear. I'm so sorry for your loss."

"Thank you. I appreciate that."

Janet ushered us into the living room where we all took seats. "Can I get you anything? Drinks? A ham sandwich? A vat of chicken and noodles?"

We all laughed. "I told you people would come out of the woodwork bearing food."

"Man, you weren't kidding. Not only that though, there were piles left over after the wake. I told all the church members that were serving to take whatever they wanted but I still ended up with a car load. I should of took it all to the station or a shelter or something. Maybe I will just pack it all up and take it with me when I go back to work on Tuesday."

"Tuesday?" we both asked her in near unison.

"Oh yeah. We have such a heavy caseload right now that I really should go back to work tomorrow but I can't.

I shot Mama a look as I asked, "Is there anything we could help you with?"

"Naw, I got it. The service is coming to get the hospital bed, the wheelchair and some of the other things some time tomorrow afternoon. I just gotta get everything cleaned up and broken down before that so they can take it away."

Mama chimed in, "Dana here has to work tomorrow but it's Marco's day to run the store. I'm usually in Zanesville in the morning doing my weekly tour of our suppliers. I could stop by and help you in the morning, if you like."

I found myself wishing she'd put that a little differently rather than making it sound like an offhand offer. Janet didn't bite on it.

"It's okay. I can handle it."

"Is it true dear, what Mel was telling us, that you're thinking of selling the place?"

She didn't seem surprised by the question. Instead, she nodded. "Yes. It's not that it's too big or anything, it isn't. It just isn't me. I lived in an apartment in city for a long time and then came back here where your neighbors are right on top of you. I liked growing up here but I never really wanted to come back here to live."

"So, when are you going to put it on the market?" I asked.

Mama answered before she could, "The sooner the better. We're moving into prime season fast. This is a lovely old Craftsman. You'll want to get it on the market quick to gin up buyer interest if you really do want to sell."

"I do. I'm not emotionally tied here. I mean, for more than nine out of the last ten years, I didn't live here."

"Then let's get the medical stuff packed up and then get this cleaned up, organized and staged. Do you know a real estate agent? If you don't, I do." Mama Chloe the steamroller. Mel had hit that one on the head after all.

Chapter 28

Dana Rossi-Crane
Late Monday Morning, March 16th, 2015

"Hey," I called poking my head into Barb's office, "Let's get out of here. Girls day out; just you and me."

"But, it's Monday. I just finished doing my ordering."

"Exactly, and now you're done. You don't have to be at the bar this evening so we don't have to watch any clocks."

"What would we do?"

"Let's go up to Amish country. We'll antique, eat lots of baked goods and just get away from all of this. Your manager is perfectly capable of handling a Monday evening."

"That's true." She looked wistful. "I suppose. Actually, I could use the break."

"Good. Grab your jacket and let's go."

"On one condition?"

"Name it."

"We don't talk about...you know...what we talked about the other day."

"You have my word."

###
Janet
Later That Same Day

Whipped beyond measure, I looked over at Chloe. At nearly twice my age, she was still going strong. We'd scrubbed and broken down all of the special equipment and moved it into the front room where it would be easy for the leasing company to retrieve it. After that, we cleaned mom's room; that is to say we scoured it from top to bottom.

I didn't have any desire to go through her clothing and toiletries and things, especially after all of that, and Aunt Leslie was tied up at her farm for the day, so Chloe volunteered to do it. There were only a few things of moms that I wanted. She set those aside for me and she made boxes for my aunts too then she went about sorting things for donation or for auction if Aunt Leslie or Rhoda decided they didn't want them either.

It was tedious work, all of it, but she didn't waver. I thought police work was tough. It didn't hold a candle to cleaning and organizing which seemed not only physically taxing but mentally too.

"Whew," Chloe finally called out after hours at it. "I could use a good cuppa. It's time for a break."

"Coffee coming right up."

"No dear; now don't you go doing that. Why don't we wash up a little and get on out of here, have a nice dinner somewhere away from all this, my treat."

"You certainly don't have to do that. You've done all of this." I spun in a quick circle waving my hand at her handiwork. "Besides, I have all that food…"

She waved me off. "Let's go somewhere and relax. That 'do gooder' food will still be here when you get back for you to keep picking at. Now then, where do you want to go? What's good around here?"

I shrugged. "There are several places within a few minutes' drive."

"Dana was telling me about a place with a funny name when we were driving over here yesterday; Muddy something. She said that's good."

"Muddy Misers. Yeah, it's really good especially if you like steaks or seafood. When my mom felt up to it, she would have me stop there and pick up a little takeout sometimes."

"Could we go there?"

"Sure. Misers it is."

###

Dana Rossi-Crane
Simultaneously, Just Outside of the Zanesville City Limits

"I'm sorry things didn't turn out quite as we planned."

"Quit apologizing; it's not your fault. We still had a nice time."

"Yes but, note to self, don't go all the way to Amish country on a Monday in the off season. Everything's closed."

We both had a little laugh at that. "Not everything," Barb said when she recovered.

"Many things, though." I had known going into the day that it would be like that. It was all part of the plan to get Barb out for a bit but then back into the area by dinner time.

"Look at the bright side," she went on, "we spent far less than we might have if we had been turned loose all day on endless antiques, cheeses, baked goods..."

"I still got fry pies, though!"

"Yes, we can't forget you and your fry pies."

"That said, I'm actually pretty hungry. It seems like I ate one of those hours ago."

"It was like, literally less than an hour," she informed me.

"Can't help it. Mama always said I have a tape worm."

"Let's stop at the bar. I'll have Joe whip you up something."

I wrinkled my nose. "No offense my friend but I'm not in the mood for burgers right now. What I could go for is a big, juicy steak."

"Mmm, that does sound good. Where should we go? I haven't been out to eat much since I've been back here since I own a bar and grill and all."

My cell buzzed. I glanced at the text quickly. It was one word from Mama, 'Go'. Bless that woman. "I know just the place" I told her.

Janet's car was in the lot across from Misers. Lucky for me, if Barb was familiar with it, she didn't seem to notice it. I drove just past the restaurant on the riverfront and parked in one of the half dozen spots beyond it.

Barb looked all around. "Kind of a dead area down here."

"After 5:00 on a Monday, yes."

"Are you sure this place is open?"

"Ha ha. Very funny." I held the door open for her and let her step inside first.

"Well, okay," she said as she took in the dark interior. "It's a bar."

"Yes and no. It's got an extensive menu and, in the summer the patio out back that overlooks the river is the place to be. It's very popular."

A hostess came up to seat us then. "Barb, party of two," I told her.

Barb turned around and gave me a funny look. She missed completely the hostess giving me a knowing one.

"Right this way. Your table is ready."

Now I got a full on inspection. "You made a reservation? In my name?'

"No big deal; I told you it's a popular place. I wanted to make sure we got a good table." I indicated she should follow the hostess and hoped by the time she processed that and dug up her next question, the game would be on. I was sweating it. I really hadn't thought this part of it out very well.

As the hostess lead us to through the main dining area toward a back corner, Mama spied us in the dim light. She stood up from the table for two where she was seated with Janet.

Barb did a double take when she spotted my mom but she couldn't hide her smile when she saw Janet. She didn't even try.

"Here Barb," Mama said, "Have a seat." She moved out of the booth, took my arm and walked us right out of the place.

"Our part's done. It's up to them to talk it out now," I said.

"Relax Dana; it worked on you and Mel, it will work on them."

"Mama, Mel collared a bank robbery suspect the night you tried this with us and left me sitting alone at that restaurant."

"Oh, that's right dear."

###
Barb

"It looks like we've been set up."

Janet craned her neck around to watch the retreating backs of Dana and Chloe then turned back to me. "Yes, I believe so."

"Dana tricked me. I see today was all a wild goose chase leading up to this."

"Chloe worked her butt off today for my part of this...whatever this is."

Taking a deep breath, I plunged in, "We really should talk about the other night."

Janet nodded. "I know...I just don't know what to say."

A server appeared and place a glass of red wine in front of each us.

"We haven't...I haven't ordered yet," I told him.

"It's all been taken care of Miss. Your salads will be out in a moment." He withdrew discreetly.

I picked up the glass and took a sip. Shrugging, I said to Janet, "It's good."

She tried hers, liked it and so we both sipped on it quietly, enjoying it until the salad course arrived. It wasn't long. Once the server disappeared again, we both started to speak.

"Go ahead," she told me.

Taking another sip for a little bit of courage I took the plunge I'd been thinking about ever since the day we nearly kissed at my house.

"We talked about Lisa, my wife, several months ago." I hesitated but she sat there waiting patiently for me to continue.

"Janet, I shut down after I lost her. I mean, I completely closed off my feelings – that whole part of myself – and I never planned on opening up like that again. We were so in love and losing her just cut me to the core.

"I understand."

Her tone was dejected. She started at her plate.

"No you don't. Not at all." I reached across the table and took her hand. "Look at me, please," I pleaded.

She finally looked up. I clasped the hand I had a hold of in both of mine. "You have made me feel things I haven't felt in the couple of years or so since Lisa's death. In fact, you made me feel some things that were even more intense than anything I ever felt with her."

"I did?"

"Yes, you did. God I loved her Janet. I still love her in all honesty but I've also come to realize that I can have more than one love in a lifetime. She's gone forever and you're here. I've felt a strong pull to you since that first night when you sat at the end of the bar and we just talked. I felt an energy with you, a connection to you, even then, but I wasn't ready for back in December. It scared me."

"And now?"

"Now...now I am."

Janet smiled and brought her other hand up to join the three already intertwined on the table.

"But," I began again.

She shuddered and started to pull both of her hand away "But, what?"

I held on. "But, I don't want to push you into something you're not ready for. You just lost your mother and..."

Janet interrupted, "I'm ready. I am so ready. I love you Barb."

"I love you too."

Smiling wide then, I looked into her eyes. I wanted to kiss her then and there and hold her forever. Instead, we were interrupted by the server discreetly clearing his throat, bearing food Chloe or Dana had ordered up in advance. We hadn't even touched the salad.

In the end, we both tucked into the meal with gusto. We needed our strength to plan out our next move and our ultimate revenge.

About the Author

Anne Hagan is an East Central Ohio based government employee by day and author by night. She and her wife live in a tiny town that's even smaller than the Morelville of her Mystery fiction novels and they wouldn't have it any other way. Anne's wife grew up there and has always considered it home. Though it's an ultra-conservative rural community, they're surrounded there by family, longtime friends and many other wonderful people with open hearts and minds. They enjoy spending time with Anne's son and his wife, with their nieces and nephews and doing many of the things you've read about in her books or that will be 'fictitiously' incorporated into future Morelville Mysteries and Cozies series books. If you've read about a hobby or a sport in either series, they probably enjoy doing it themselves or someone very close to them does.

Anne and her wife are the co-owners of a haunted house: Hagan's House of Horrors. Much as her dream has always been to write fiction, her spouse's dream has been to create it through the medium of horror. They took their haunt operation fully commercial in 2015. Watch them as they grow!

Broken Women is Anne's ninth book but her first romance. If you enjoyed this book and you also like mysteries with a touch of romance, please consider the lesbian fiction Morelville Mysteries series that features Sheriff Mel, Dana and several others at least mentioned in this story. Also, if you're interested in cozy mystery stories, please consider reading <u>The Passed Prop</u>, the first book in the spin off Morelville Cozies series by Anne that features meddling mothers Faye Crane and Chloe Rossi in a case only they could solve. Future stories are planned for both series.

As always, thank you for reading!

Also Written by the Author

Relic: The Morelville Mysteries – Book 1 –
The first Dana and Sheriff Mel mystery and the
first book in the Morelville saga. ***It is widely
available as a free download wherever
eBooks are sold.*** Please click the link above
which will take you to Anne's website where you
can obtain a link to get the book at your retailer
of choice.

**Cases collide for two star crossed
ladies of law enforcement...**

Customs Special Agent Dana Rossi was
forced to start her life anew after a bad breakup
with her former girlfriend and the loss of job
that she loved. These days, she spends life on the
road, moving from one case to another until one
day when runs run right into the path of Sheriff

Mel Crane. The feisty, sexy butch cop is as determined to uncover a counterfeiting ring in her county as Agent Rossi becomes to stop a stalker obsessed with Mel and hot for her company. Dana is under the added pressure of conducting an undercover investigation of her own with a tight deadline: finding and then stopping a ring of smugglers bringing high end designer knock-offs into the states.

Could their cases be related? When repeated vicious attacks on Mel and on her home accelerate the danger for her *and also* their attraction to each other, they become desperate to find the truth and solve the two mysteries. Can they find a way to work together to resolve both cases while coming to terms with their growing feelings for one another? Can Dana move beyond her jilted lover past and find true happiness with a small town Sheriff?

<u>Busy Bees: The Morelville Mysteries – Book 2</u>

Romance and Murder Mix in the Latest Story Featuring Sheriff Mel Crane and Special Agent Dana Rossi!

Customs Special Agent Dana Rossi is down but not out after being shot and seriously injured during her previous assignment. Will romance blossom or will sparks fly when she agrees to shack up in Morelville with the beautiful butch Sheriff Melissa 'Mel' Crane and her extended family while she recovers?

Will murder get in the way of love? If murder doesn't, will life in a house with children or a political campaign keep them apart? Can Mel solve two major crimes and keep her former job on the road loving girlfriend happy in a tiny town?

Dana's Dilemma: The Morelville Mysteries – Book 3 – The relationship matures between Mel and Dana in an installment that features a breaking Amish character, an ex-girlfriend, a conniving politician and murder.

Elections and Old Loves Combine with Deadly Results in the Newest Romantic Mystery Featuring Sheriff Mel Crane and Special Agent Dana Rossi!

What happens when Mel runs for Sheriff, an Amish girl runs away from home and Dana runs – er, limps - for cover? Can anything else possibly go wrong for these two ladies of law enforcement? Sure it can and it will!

Can the two sometimes lovers work it all out once and for all and finally have a happy life together or will more crime, murder and mayhem get in the way?

Hitched and Tied: The Morelville Mysteries – Book 4

Mel and Dana attempt to bring their growing romantic relationship full circle but family, duty and family duties all conspire to get in the way.

A victim with close ties to the Cranes escapes a deadly assault with his life only to die from his injuries minutes later. Mel has few clues to find the fighter turned murderer and the further she goes with her investigation, the more the situation deteriorates. Meanwhile, Dana's trying to plan their wedding but the family is resisting both her efforts and the wishes of the couple while focusing more on her sister and her traditional relationship.

Family angst, violent crime and more than a few Holstein steers abound as Dana and Mel fight against the odds to solve Mel's case and find their own happily ever after.

Viva Mama Rossi!: The Morelville Mysteries – Book 5 – The 5th tale in the Morelville Mysteries and the book that gives fans a full introduction to future Morelville Cozies series sleuths Faye Crane (Mel's mom) and Chloe Rossi (Dana's Mama). The two series stand-alone but they're certainly better together. For just the back story on Faye and Chloe and how they came to team up to solve mysteries, <u>Viva Mama Rossi!</u> is a quick and entertaining read. The synopsis:

A delayed honeymoon getaway takes a deadly turn for newlyweds Mel and Dana; meanwhile, two meddling mothers won't let sleeping fisherman lie in the latest Morelville Mystery.

Does an unsolved shooting death far away from Morelville have local ties? Did a fisherman really drown or was there something more sinister afloat?

All Mel and Dana wanted was to enjoy a nice, relaxing honeymoon in the Smokey Mountains, away from the strains of life in the public eye. Instead, they end up involved in a case local law enforcement has completely written off. Things are no better back home where their own mothers are stirring up an all-new hornets' nest that they think Mel and her own department have written off.

If there is going to be any rest for anyone, something is going to have to break in one case or the other...

A Crane Christmas: The Morelville Mysteries – Book 6

Is it the Christmas season or the 'silly season'?

All Sheriff Mel wants to do is close out the year and spend a joyful first Christmas with Dana and with their extended families. She's even hired a new detective, Janet Mason, to ease some of the workload for her and her only other detective, Shane Harding. Things were shaping up great for her and Dana for a relaxing holiday season. Too bad it just wasn't meant to be...

The local criminals want it all too and a string of burglaries in high class county enclaves have Mel and both of her detectives stymied. Throw in a bunch of disappearing dogs, some designer sheep, a lonely woman and an unsolved murder case, and the good guys are at their wits end. Meanwhile, back in tiny little Morelville, things aren't much better; the village is buzzing over Dana's family taking over the store but Dana herself isn't so sure that's a good thing.

Can Mel and her team resolve everything before Christmas dinner comes out of the oven? Will Janet Mason fit in at all? Will Dana find a balance between work and family that works for her in time to enjoy her first Christmas with Mel?

Mad for Mel: The Morelville Mysteries – Book 7

Rival gangs will stop at nothing to gain sole control of the drug trade in Muskingum County and they've picked Valentine's week to create a firestorm of murder and mayhem as they battle each other for supremacy.

Sheriff Mel Crane is blindsided by looting, murdering and marauding bikers at a time of year when most Harley's are tucked safely away from the effects of Ohio winters that come rife with snow and ice. They're rolling out, they're out of control and she can't stop them. On the home front, she's feeling guilty about spending so much time working and hardly any time with Dana, especially when she knows Valentine's Day is right around the corner...or so her mother-in-law keeps reminding her.

Dana just wants Mel to be safe; she has her own problems to worry about. Her attempt at novel writing isn't going as well as she hoped and she's bored. She got a little taste of what it was like to be an investigator again and she misses it. What to do?

Hannah's Hope: The Morelville Mysteries – Book 8

A young mother with a troubled past seeks help from Mel and Dana but is their effort to assist her too little, too late?

Hannah Yoder appears on Dana and Mel's doorstep late one night with her teenage friend Katie and Katie's newborn baby in tow telling the couple the girl and child are in trouble and have no place else to go. Dana and Mel offer refuge for the night and a firm promise to talk about the future. Plans are barely made when first one mysterious tragedy strikes and then another leaving Mel, Dana, Hannah and the Crane and Rossi families with few clues and little hope.

Mel knows there's a killer out there; she just doesn't know where to start looking. She's stonewalled at every turn and running out of time. Somebody knows something that will unlock the mysteries swirling all around, but who?

The Passed Prop: The Morelville Cozies – Book 1 – The first book in the Morelville Cozies series featuring meddling mother sleuths Faye Crane and Chloe Rossi.

Chloe Rossi wants to retire with her husband and move away from suburban sprawl to bucolic Morelville; the only

trouble is, Morelville is experiencing its worst crime wave ever and Marco Rossi wants no part of a move there. What to do?

Faye Crane would like nothing more than to have her good friend Chloe move closer to her and to Chloe's own daughter. She's got Chloe convinced it's a smart move but Marco is a tougher nut to crack. A string of brutal crimes around Halloween with no witnesses and little evidence to work with has her own Sheriff daughter and her entire department stymied. Marco is second guessing even taking his retirement since Sheriff Mel can't get a handle on it all and bring peace and well-being back to the tiny village.

Someone has to root out a killer. Can Faye and Chloe nose around and figure out what the police can't to solve the crime? If they do, will Marco still waver or will he consent to move?

This is the first book in a spin off series from the Morelville Mysteries series by Anne Hagan. The book stands alone but, if you're interested in getting all of the Crane and Rossi families back story, you should check out the fifth book in the first series, <u>Viva Mama Rossi!</u>.

<u>Opera House Ops: The Morelville Cozies –</u>
<u>Book 2</u> – This began releasing in serial form, one
episode a week, in late August of 2016.

**Sinister goings-on at a vacant 1800's
era opera house in Morelville have the
residents of the village all tied up in knots
and Faye Crane trying to solve multiple
crimes and playing savior to history.**

**A Morelville Cozies Serial Mystery:
Episode 1 – Breaking In**

Faye Crane and Chloe Rossi are back in the
latest Morelville cozy mystery. Multiple strange
occurrences at a Morelville village landmark
have them back in crime fighting mode only to
find out there's far more going on with the old
'opera house' than first meets the eye.

**This serial mystery is great together with
Book 1 of The Morelville Cozy series, The
Passed Prop, to get all of the Crane and
Rossi families back story but it can also
be read as a stand-alone mystery.**

~~~

Three multi-eBook boxed sets of the works of Anne Hagan are also available for purchase.

The Morelville Collection is an eight eBook set that includes all of the full length Morelville Mysteries novels featuring Sheriff Melissa 'Mel' Crane and Special Agent Dana Rossi. It is currently available exclusively at Amazon for the Kindle and via Kindle Unlimited.

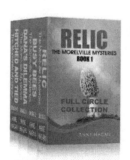 

The Morelville Mysteries Full Circle Collection is a five eBook set that contains the first four Morelville Mysteries novels and an exclusive <u>Companion Guide</u> that is only available with this set. The set is available for $3.99 at multiple outlets. Most carry it with the 3D cover on the left. Apple iTunes/iBooks does not allow 3D cover views so it's available there with the more generic cover on the right. Please click the hyperlink just above for a page at Anne's website where you can get links to all the retailers who carry this set.

<u>The Morelville Mysteries: Books 5-8 Collection</u> is a four eBook set that contains the most recent additions to the ongoing Morelville Mysteries series. The set is available for $3.99 at multiple outlets. Please click the hyperlink just above for a page at Anne's website where you can get links to all the retailers who carry this set.

Check Anne Out on her blog, on Facebook or on Twitter:

For the latest information about upcoming releases, other projects, sample chapters and everything personal, check out Anne's **blog** at https://AnneHaganAuthor.com/ or like Anne on **Facebook** at https://www.facebook.com/AuthorAnneHagan. You can also connect with Anne on **Twitter** @AuthorAnneHagan.

Made in the USA
Columbia, SC
11 June 2017